Dying at the Pub

Beatrice Fishback

eLectio Publishing
Little Elm, TX
www.eLectioPublishing.com

Dying to Eat at the Pub
By Beatrice Fishback

Copyright 2016 by Beatrice Fishback. All rights reserved.
Cover Design by eLectio Publishing. All rights reserved.

ISBN-13: 978-1-63213-310-6
Published by eLectio Publishing, LLC
Little Elm, Texas
http://www.eLectioPublishing.com

Printed in the United States of America

5 4 3 2 1 eLP 20 19 18 17 16

The eLectio Publishing editing team is comprised of: Christine LePorte, Lori Draft, Sheldon James, Court Dudek, and Kaitlyn Campbell.

Without limiting the rights under copyright reserved above, no part of this publication may be reproduced, stored in or introduced into a retrieval system, or transmitted, in any form, or by any means (electronic, mechanical, photocopying, recording, or otherwise), without the prior written permission of both the copyright owner and the above publisher of this book.

If you purchased this book without a cover, you should be aware that this book is stolen property. It was reported as "unsold and destroyed" to the publisher and neither the author nor the publisher has received any payment for the "stripped book."

The scanning, uploading, and distribution of this book via the Internet or via any other means without the permission of the publisher is illegal and punishable by law. Please purchase only authorized electronic editions, and do not participate in or encourage electronic piracy of copyrighted materials. Your support of the author's rights is appreciated.

Publisher's Note
The publisher does not have any control over and does not assume any responsibility for author or third-party websites or their content.

This is a work of fiction. Names, characters, places, and incidents either are the product of the author's imagination or are used fictitiously, and any resemblance to actual persons, living or dead, business establishments, events, or locales is entirely coincidental.

Acknowledgments

To my Jim: Thanks for making marriage delightfully cozy and often mysteriously wonderful. I can't imagine life without you.

To friends who made this story possible: Elizabeth Tyrrell, British editor and friend par excellence.

Linda Robinson, Irene Onorato and Dana K. Ray, Janet Lindquist and Heidi Barnes. This book wouldn't be the same without you.

Dying to Eat at the Pub

Chapter One

The glint of a safari hunter reflected in his eyes. "Don't ever forget what happened last time, Dotty Weathervane." Out the door he went with his sharp, pitchforked tools.

Fresh spring air swished around my ankles, and a tremor rippled up the keyboard of my spine.

Enough said. I knew exactly what he meant. Memories are a funny thing though. Each person walks away with a different point of view. This series of events proved to be no exception.

+ + +

It all began as it normally did with my morning routine: several cups of dark European java. Coffee so thick you could cut and serve it as an appetizer. I inhaled the thick, dark bouquet of steaming liquid in my chipped, but much loved, Queen Elizabeth Golden Jubilee cup.

I stuck my face further into the mug. "Mirror, mirror, in a cup, tell me I'm fairer than the neighbor's pup." I chuckled at the swishing liquid and swallowed another long, delicious mouthful as steam misted heavenward. It was a good thing coffee couldn't speak. On second thought, this one had just spoken volumes.

Jim clucked his tongue and held the morning paper higher. Unlike me, my retired husband's routine began with his favorite beverage, a cup of Earl Grey—generally considered an afternoon drink by tea connoisseurs—and either the local paper or *The Independent*.

My "coffee mirror" viewing all these years had obviously taken a toll on his nerves. Marriage truly was a longtime testing ground for spouses—similar to the testing grounds the military used for nuclear warheads. In either case you never knew when an explosion might happen.

I swallowed one last bite of soggy muesli. "It's great you don't have to rush out for work anymore, isn't it?"

The paper swished.

Well, at least he's still breathing behind there.

An advertisement for Marks and Spencer—also known as M&S by the British—faced me, and boasted a half-price sale of handbags and clothing coming soon.

Young, petite models wearing skimpy tops and skirts resembling tutus held the M&S logo in their outstretched hands.

"Wonder what I'd look like in one of those outfits." Probably like Hyacinth Hippo in Disney's *Fantasia*.

The paper bobbed up and down.

"I love being able to relax in the mornings, don't you, Jim?" As the paper danced in his hand, my head jounced in rhythm as I tried to mentally note the dates of the sale.

I spoke into the cup. "Sure would like it if he talked more. Since he's retired from the military, he hardly speaks at all." The words echoed back.

"I know," Jim said through the printed page.

"You mean you heard me?"

Down the paper went, and the advert models collapsed. "I've heard everything you've said."

Up the paper went.

Jim might not say much, but I thought of us as two well-worn slippers—a little tattered and scruffy, but an old, comfortable pair nonetheless.

Sometimes when I looked at him, I saw the young, attractive man I married some forty-odd years ago. Then there were days like today. The stubble on his morning face, faded green shirt, and torn denim trousers a testimony to the casual wear he had chosen for the "golden years." Bruce Willis—*R.E.D. Retired Extremely Dangerous*—he was not.

He wasn't the only thing messy around here either. If our kitchen got any more cluttered, we wouldn't be able to find the cutlery for our next meal.

Jim crumpled the paper. "What's the world coming to, Dotty? There's been a murder right here in East Lark."

His announcement obscured the disorder and put a blinding halt to our breakfast as the aroma of burnt multi-grain toast stifled the air.

"What? Who? Let me see." I tugged part of the paper from his garden-calloused hands. "Do you think this is going to put the village on the global map or worldwide web?"

Although I hadn't been awake long, I was alert enough to know: I hoped not. East Lark, an English village with two pubs, a village shop, and three churches each with a congregation of about five, was our chosen place for retirement. We loved the quiet serenity, and I wanted it to stay that way.

Jim gulped the last of his cooled Earl Grey and shrugged. "Not sure. And we can't get involved either, Dot." His last word snapped like a single gunshot.

I ignored him and flipped to the next page. "The last thing we want is a place swarming with news reporters or thrill-seekers in search of a change of scenery."

My eyes tried to focus as I drew the newspaper closer. "Where are my reading glasses?" A leopard-patterned pair lay buried under the rest of the scattered newspaper on the pine-topped table. I slid them onto the tip of my nose.

Jim took his cup to the sink and headed toward the back door. "I'm going out to the garden." He grabbed an assortment of tools more conducive to slashing and dashing through a jungle than implements suitable to our small garden and hanging baskets.

I scanned the paper and waited for the back door to shut. Instead, a cool spring breeze swam around my ankles and tickled up my legs.

I flipped the edge of the headlines down.

Jim's free hand held the doorknob. "Dotty Weathervane, I don't want you getting *any* ideas about getting involved with this murder."

"What can you possibly mean?"

"Remember what happened the last time you tried your hand at being a private eye?" His lifted eyebrow resembled a question mark.

Putting the paper down, I picked up my coffee and slouched in the chair, trying to act nonchalant. "Thought you'd forgotten about that. It was ages ago."

His other eyebrow went up in precision arch with the first. "How could I possibly forget about the soldier whose wife killed him, especially since I was his company commander? So let me remind *you*, you were so embroiled in the whole mess it nearly cost you your life and me my job."

"Well, how was I to know she was fed up with her husband and hated being a military wife with all the moving and whatnot? I couldn't possibly know she was a cold-blooded killer, could I? All I wanted to do was help." I flicked the tips of my fingers in the air with a brush stroke, picked up the news, and pretended to scan the headlines.

Cool air continued to swish around my feet.

I set the paper down and removed my glasses. "What?" Impatience edged its way into my tone.

Jim moved his tools from one arm to the other. "That's the problem, Dotty. All you ever want to do is help. Then you end up getting yourself in trouble. The woman nearly killed you when she discovered you were on to her." He pulled in his chin and softened his tone. "I don't want anything to happen to you, that's all."

Enough said. Out the door he went with his tools and gardening attire, my safari hunter heading into his jungle of an English garden.

Chapter Two

"You're right, Jim. I shouldn't get involved," I mumbled.

Through the large French kitchen door windows, I could see him squat and peer at his bed of baby seedlings and plants.

With flat palms, I pushed myself up from the table.

"Guess I really can't do anything about this murder anyway." The kitchen mess still glared at me with evil intent.

Each morning I picked things up and put them away. The next day the chaos reappeared as if a magician had waved his magic wand and tossed everything into mayhem during the night. This morning there were several piles of stacked mail, a mound of dishes in the sink, newspapers, and a variety of other items scattered everywhere. At least it was all hidden under a layer of fine white fairy dust—what others might call dirt.

I was determined to straighten up the clutter even if it took all day.

Putting the paper and coffee aside, I wrapped my pink-mottled Laura Ashley apron—a gift from my best friend, Kate—around my rather full frame and swept the burnt toast crumbs off the counter into the circular, silver trash can.

A moment later I stopped, slid off my right shoe, and relieved a grateful bunion. Leaning on the kitchen counter, I twisted my toes. Snap. Crackle. Pop. The Rice Krispies cereal "pop" was a peep compared to the racket my "piggies" made. I delayed at the countertop and considered the headline news.

Clop . . . clop . . . clop . . . clop. The sounds of a horse passed along the front of the house and snapped me out of my reverie.

What used to be farm country with workhorses was now a place for horse lovers to canter down country lanes. The first time I saw bags of horse manure near various driveways offered for sale for a mere fifty pence, I had to chuckle. Guess it was good fertilizer.

But there were many folks who offered a lot of free horse manure without anyone even asking for it.

I slipped the too-tight shoe back on, wiped down the oak counter, and began throwing things into oversized recycling bags by the back door, all the while humming "Slip Slidin' Away." Paul Simon was fab and the words of his seventies song seemed rather appropriate for the moment.

One recycle bag was piled sky high with plastics. I collapsed some of the containers to make more room, threw in the morning paper and my favorite chick magazine, *Break*, and gave my attention to the dishes in the sink.

The accumulation of heaped blue and white china in the stainless steel basin appeared more like an erupted volcano than classic English Spode. Glued food stuck to each piece.

The dishes were overwhelming. Instead, I grabbed a sack of recycled paper to lug outside. Page one of the morning news sat perched on top like a child's folded birthday hat with a name in bold letters.

I snatched out the paper, put my back to the garden and Jim's viewpoint of the kitchen. If he had any inkling I was checking out more information about the murder he would raise those bushy eyebrows to the top of his balding head and give me "the look."

Grabbing my glasses, I shimmied down to the floor and sat on my haunches, hiding behind the counter.

What I hadn't noticed earlier was the name of the person they found stabbed to death in the Queen's Treat dumpster—what the villagers would call a skip. The Queen's Treat, with its skeletal queen holding a scepter pub sign, was the place the young folks went for karaoke and a pint. The Hare and Hound pub, on the other hand, was the family favorite place to eat.

The name of the dead man in the dumpster was an American named Dan Swansey, husband to US Air Force Captain Barbara Swansey.

Several hundred US military members lived in East Lark and worked on an American air base abutting the village. Although the blending of British and American cultures could at times be strained, at other times no one would ever guess there were two nations merged into one small community.

What would this murder do for public relations? As I flicked the paper open to the second page, an editorial confirmed my suspicions and revealed it wouldn't be good:

"There was a time when cultural tensions were running rampant in our area. Those who lived in East Lark a decade ago might remember how two American soldiers attacked a local lad during a summer beer festival at the banger-racing course. Many have forgotten the ill feelings the incident incurred. With an American dead in the village, could this recharge those bad feelings?"

Oh, dear. What a shame.

And what a shame it was Dan Swansey who was killed. I didn't know him personally, but I knew he and Barbara moved into the village only six months ago.

Bliiiing.

The phone's ringing made me leap from my crouched position and I hit my head on the overhanging lip of the counter. I had been concentrating so intently on the article I'd become oblivious to reality—of course, at my age that seemed to occur quite regularly.

Rubbing the now growing bump, yet still entranced by the paper's details, I picked up the phone. "East Lark, 58 1808."

"Dotty, this is Kate. Have you seen the morning papers? Did you know Dan Swansey was murdered? And did you see the part about how he was left in the pub's dumpster?" Kate's eloquent British accent sang with each question. Even after the almost eight years I'd known her, Kate's voice still reminded me of Julie

Andrews as she flitted across the Austrian terrain in *The Sound of Music*.

"Mmmm," was all I could muster to my best friend.

A harsh *rap, rap, rap* made me jump. Jim's pressed face with curled fingers wrapped around his eyes peered through the paned window. I quickly crumpled the paper, tossed it aside, and grabbed my Queen mug.

These distractions were more than my heart could take. Jim had finished his tea but I was only working on my second cup of coffee. On average, I needed a full pot to get going.

In my hurried attempt to get rid of the paper and grab my drink, I nearly dropped the cup. "Yes, Kate, I just read it." I set the mug down with a harder thunk than intended. Coffee spit out, leaving dark brown spots on my Ashley apron and the kitchen floor.

Jim continued rapping on the windowpane, mouthing unintelligible words, the watering can dangling in his other hand.

"Kate, can I call you back?" I hung up, tossed the newspaper back into the recycling bag, opened the back door, and stepped outside. Jim still peered in the kitchen window.

"Jim."

He spun my way, giving me a sheepish look.

"Why are you tapping on the window? What could you possibly want? I was on the phone. Couldn't you see me?" My questions resembled a machine gun set on rapid fire. The poor fellow didn't have a chance to answer the first question before I volleyed the next.

"Dotty, I need some water. And no, I couldn't see you were on the phone. The sun's reflection in the window made it impossible."

Whew. At least he didn't see me reading the paper.

"Then how did you know I was even in here?"

"Just knew." To say Jim was a man of few words would be an understatement, like saying the *Titanic* had a small leak. It's one trait I found loveable about him since I was generally the talker in the relationship and Jim the nodding listener. Although more often than not, when he was nodding I didn't think he was necessarily listening.

"Can't you use the tap outside?" I asked.

"No hot water out here. I need warm water for this special fertilizer." He thrust the gray, metallic watering can into my hand and walked away. My arm nearly pulled out of its socket. Even without liquid the thing weighed a ton.

Low-lying clouds hung overhead and the smell of moisture in the air attested to another morning of rain.

I set the can down. "The weather doesn't look very favorable."

With a back wave of his hand he retreated to the bedding plants in the far corner of the garden. Time taught me he hadn't really heard what I'd said.

Now that Jim had discovered gardening and dreamed of being Alan Titchmarsh, he seemed to need my help in every detail of life including fetching warm water. How he managed to get by all those years as a military man without me standing right beside him was beyond my imagination.

Jim's hero, Alan Titchmarsh, had an advantage over him. He'd started gardening at the age of ten in his parents' Yorkshire back garden. Jim had only been at it for a few years. Mr. Titchmarsh had wooed television viewers as a host for *Love Your Garden*. His baby-faced, winsome smile even made me want to try my hand at tilling the soil.

Empty pots were scattered haphazardly around our yard, tools tossed hither and yon, and a rake tossed in the grass resembled an oversized salad fork. In spite of the cost, I was glad Jim had discovered the hobby. But his luck with growing things was hit-or-miss and the weather always seemed to be against him. Maybe this would be his lucky year.

I lugged the can into the kitchen, determined to get back to clearing up the mess.

Walking past the recycling bag with the crumpled morning paper still on top, I tightly closed my eyes.

I can't get involved. I can't get involved.

I reopened one eye, hoping the paper had disintegrated, the mess had magically disappeared, and I was on some idyllic island with waving palm trees, sipping a cool fruit juice with one of those little umbrellas and cherries sitting atop—and Don Ho singing "Tiny Bubbles" in the background. No such luck.

Instead of heading to the sink, I plunked the water bucket down and grabbed the paper. As much as I liked the quietness of the village, a little excitement was good for my soul.

I poured another cup of coffee, sat on a stool, slid off both shoes, and reminisced about the first time I met Captain Barbara Swansey—wife to the dead man in the dumpster. We'd met briefly in the village shop only a few months before.

Chapter Three

In the shop I was used to seeing US military people in uniform. But a certain patch on this young woman's jacket intrigued me.

"Good morning. I'm Dotty Weathervane. Are you new to East Lark?" I grabbed a small red-handled basket for purchases.

"Why yes, I'm Barbara Swansey." A newspaper was tucked under one arm, and a military hat dangled from her hand. "I was recently assigned here. It's nice to meet you."

Her accent caught my attention. "Where are you from, Barbara?" I placed teacakes in the basket along with two bags of salt and vinegar crisps—Jim's favorite potato chips.

"I'm from Long Island," the emphasis being on "Long."

"Ah, I thought I recognized it. I'm originally from upstate New York."

"Really?"

I glanced at the price sticker on a carton of milk. "What? Oh yes. But I've lived away from New York a long time. Although, hearing you makes me homesick." My vivid lemon-lime handbag that Jim called a suitcase slid down my shoulder and landed on the crook of my arm. I yanked it back up.

Barbara's smile was warm and friendly. "I'm sure you don't miss the traffic, smog, or the crime."

The bell on the shop door rang shrilly. Several folks came in and out for their fresh bread, free-range eggs, and other sundry items.

The village shop, though small, sold a large variety of local fare. Crammed into a space reminiscent of an American-sized walk-in closet were various cereals, breads, and a brown paper-lined shelf filled with fresh fruits and vegetables. Purchasing stamps and posting mail was also available. Best of all, I learned everything I needed to know about what was going on in the village in a matter of minutes.

DYING TO EAT AT THE PUB

Erika, an American gal who lived next door to us, entered carrying her newborn baby strapped in a Mothercare bundle. Her long blond hair swished back and forth across her back like a sweeping broom. She bounced past us and smiled.

Barbara and I shuffled further into the corner, away from the cool breeze that flitted early spring petals from nearby flowering trees into the entryway.

The flow of foot traffic slowed, and my conversation with Barbara returned to her assignment in England.

"My husband, Dan, and I are so excited to be here." Her green eyes flashed with animation and her bright teeth glittered. I expected to hear a "ping" on her top tooth, perfect for a Crest commercial. "We've been married only a few years, and this is like being on an extended honeymoon. We can't wait to have the chance to travel around Europe."

"Is Dan from New York too?"

"No, California."

"How does a girl from New York meet a guy from California?" Having been a military wife for many years I knew there was a multitude of ways two people from the opposite sides of America could meet.

"Dan was in the military. We were both stationed at the Defense Language Institute in California. In fact, he was my instructor." A sweep of pink blushed across her freckled nose and cheeks. "Once he finished his commitment, he resigned from the service. But I still have to serve a few more years." She lowered her voice and glanced around the shop. "This village is pretty quiet though, and it's hard to meet people."

I put the basket down and dug in my handbag for my deeply buried wallet. "I'm sure you'll grow to love it. The villagers are friendly, once you get to know them." I didn't want to discourage her by adding it could take years to break the ice with some of them. "The wide-open farm fields have a special beauty, too." I pulled out a crinkled five-pound note to pay. "I must warn you, though, there's nothing quite like the sweet smell of leeks being harvested." I wrinkled my nose in jest and gave her a cheeky smile.

"I'm so used to being in the middle of a city it might take me some time to adjust."

"You'll get used to it." She'd find out soon enough how unquiet the place actually was during certain times of the year. "Wait 'til you hear the jets running their engines at five in the morning. Or see the hundreds of folks called 'bird watchers' who flock here during the late summer holidays. They make detailed records of the different types of military planes taking off and landing. It's a hobby I've never quite understood."

I walked beside her to the checkout. "I hope you and Dan enjoy your time here." Collecting my change, I stood aside as she paid for her purchases.

"Have a nice day, Barbara. It was nice meeting you. I hope to see you again soon." We left the shop going in two different directions—she toward a sparkling red BMW Z-3 parked curbside while I headed home.

I waved as she zipped past.

Drats, I forgot to ask about the patch on her uniform.

+ + +

As weeks went by, I saw Barbara less and heard more about Dan's shenanigans at the pub. Rumor at the village shop was that a game of darts in the Queen's Treat had escalated into a brawl. The rumor mill also had it that Dan and Barbara's marriage was on the rocks.

Could his death have been caused by an argument with her?

I tried to visualize Barbara with menacing eyes, swinging a machete and hurling Dan sky-high into the dumpster. Of course, the last time I assumed a wife was innocent of murder I was way off base. In this case I couldn't see it. Not with Barbara's soft, lovely green eyes, gentle face, and a body like a Barbie doll. In fact, she made her uniform look quite attractive, which was hard to do with baggy desert camouflage fatigues and combat boots.

No, Barbara couldn't possibly be on the list of suspects, could she? But how much did I really know about her? We'd only exchanged a few conversations. And she was always evasive whenever I asked about her job in the military.

Wonder what she's hiding?

+ + +

Perched on the kitchen stool with my apron twisted sideways, I stood, shifted the apron to its proper place, and sat back down. One day, Weight Watchers and I might meet on the road to the bakery shop, but I doubted it.

After two more cups of joe and reading the rest of the paper, I felt perkier. I put my shoes back on, slid off the stool, and started where I'd left off.

"Heigh-ho, heigh-ho," I whistled and carried recycle bags outside, returned, and put various things away in cupboards. The kitchen was becoming presentable, and I was seeing light at the end of the clutter.

When the kitchen was clean, it was a beautiful room. The open floor plan and large windows faced the garden and made it light and airy. Pale green coloring on the walls—like sea foam at the Felixstowe coast—made the normally dismal days of winter brighter.

Other portions of the house were built over two hundred and fifty years ago and at one time it was a pub for the locals. A set of worn brick steps led down to an old beer cellar. I imagined many a brutish man lugging barrels up and down them during the Victorian era when prosperity dominated the upper class.

I made one last broad stroke of the broom across the hardwood floor and clapped my hands at a job well done. There was enough space in the sink to begin filling Jim's watering can.

As the water ran, I returned Kate's call.

We jumped back into our previous conversation as if we hadn't skipped a beat. "Do you think Barbara Swansey could've been involved with the murder of her husband?" I asked.

"I don't know either one of them very well, but Dan Swansey sure seemed to cause problems wherever he went. In fact, the last time I saw him outside the village shop he was arguing with Arty for some reason."

"Hmm, wonder why Arty?"

Arty Smith, our rather obscure postman, began delivering mail last year, taking over when John Edwards retired. Although we had exchanged a few polite comments when we met at the shop, I didn't know much about him.

I reached to turn off the tap and splashed water everywhere. "Guess Dan picked a fight wherever he went."

Holding the phone between my chin and shoulder, I grabbed a brand new crimson tea towel. Tossing the cloth to the floor, I held it in place with one foot and swabbed up a few drops. "Think I'll call Barbara Swansey and try to arrange a visit. Maybe I can find out firsthand what was going on with her and Dan. I'm curious what kind of marriage they really had."

The red tea towel made the water turn into a pink puddle.

"Ahem."

I hesitated—then looked over my right shoulder.

Jim stood shadowed in the doorway. He took one step inside. The deep rutted frown on his forehead, thin pursed lips, and balled fists on his hips told me he'd heard plenty of my conversation. He'd warned me not to get involved and here I was planning a visit to the dead man's house to question his widow about their marriage.

"I wondered why you were taking so long getting water for me." With raised eyebrows, giving me "the look" and a shake of his head, he clucked his tongue and went back out the door.

"I better go, Kate. Something's come up."

What had gone up was Jim's blood pressure.

Chapter Four

Jim was generally an easygoing guy.

However, when I pushed the wrong buttons I was liable to be checked on the next space shuttle to the moon. Maybe now was the time to start packing my bags.

While trying to formulate what to say to Jim, the phone rang yet again.

"East Lark, 58 1808."

"Dotty. This is Lillie. Have you seen the paper?" The words zipped through the phone faster than a Singer sewing machine whizzed through fabric.

News got around a small village quicker than anywhere else. The paper, telly, and Internet had nothing compared to village folks, the local shop, and one woman in East Lark named Lillie Bakersfield. Give the information to her and the whole region knew within minutes.

"Hello, Lillie," I replied, a bit more sarcastically than intended. I had firsthand experience of her expertise in gossip when we first moved to the village eight years ago.

A few days after we'd settled into our new home she had invited me out for tea.

+ + +

Sipping and sharing go hand-in-hand when you're in a teashop, and I did both with gusto on my first visit to Molly's Tea Leaf with Lillie. The shop, in a nearby village, had the reputation of serving the best scones in Suffolk. They did not lie.

A black menu board hung on the wall and boasted its specialties, including homemade cakes, soup, and a plethora of sandwiches.

The chunky waitress, in her black Victorian dress and white apron, looked more like an overstuffed penguin instead of an elegant reminder of days gone by. The puffed sleeves on her blouse squeezed her fleshy arms into what resembled upside down muffins.

Our "penguin" waddled over with our tea and food order: two large, sultana-filled scones for me and a slice of carrot cake for Lillie, the cream cheese frosting on her cake nearly an inch thick.

Artistically, I slathered clotted cream over the face of a scone like Rembrandt creating a masterpiece. Lillie watched as I plopped a spoon of homemade raspberry jam atop the cream.

When the masterpiece was complete, I took a bite into the decadent work of art and felt the cool cream slide along my face. A swipe with a serviette and a swallow of tea completed the whole creative experience.

My sweet tooth was completely satisfied.

I gazed out the window overlooking the teashop garden. "Why is it so difficult to drive here? I think the problem is I can't seem to master the steering column on the right-hand side of the car."

Lillie listened, wide-eyed as a night owl.

"When I first drove our new car here I hit a curb and popped a tire, pushing the alignment out of whack. Jim was not happy with me, I can tell you."

"Give yourself time, Dotty. You'll be fine."

"And roundabouts? They're a nightmare. I always want to drive the wrong way on them. Who'd think it could be so hard?"

During the entire time Lillie merely nodded with a look of concern etched along her long, thin face.

We finished our time at Molly's Tea Leaf and headed home.

Driving along the narrow lane, I smacked the tires on the verge with a thump-da-de-thump to avoid a flashing red pheasant dashing to and fro in front of the vehicle like a crazed roadrunner. The experience verified everything I'd shared over tea about my ineptitude at driving a car in England.

Next thing I knew everyone in East Lark was joking about needing to stay off the street when they saw me behind the wheel of a car.

Ever since, I had been pretty careful about what I shared with Lillie.

+++

"Dotty, Dotty, are you still there?"

I shook my head and came back to my senses while Lillie continued chattering on the phone.

"Yes, I'm still here."

"Dotty, you and Jim *must* come to the village hall this evening. I've called together a Neighborhood Watch meeting. Since this dreadful murder happened, *no one* is safe in East Lark. No one, I tell you."

Did I mention Lillie also had an overactive imagination? Because one man was found dead in a dumpster she was sure that by morning the entire village would be like the one in the *Dawn of the Dead* film about a group of zombies preying on humans.

I wondered what the others in the village were saying about Dan and Barbara. It had been proven in the past that everything they said would be blown way out of proportion. But there was only one way to find out. Go to the village hall.

I exhaled slowly. "Okay, Lillie, Jim and I will be there if I can drag him out of his garden. He wants to finish planting before the rain starts up again."

And he may want to throttle me with some stinging nettle too.

After Jim had overheard my conversation with Kate earlier—the one where I was planning a visit to Barbara Swansey—I doubted he would want to go anywhere with me.

"What time's the meeting?" I asked.

Lillie deepened her voice and spoke as if she had the authority of a police officer. "Half past seven. Now ... be sure to bring a knife or something to defend yourself on the way to and from the meeting in case you're accosted by someone."

This suggestion was ludicrous even coming from her since she knew we lived directly across the street from the village hall.

Lillie hung up. Amazingly, the conversation was short and to the point, not always the case with her.

Right now I had better things to do than chat on the phone, such as coming up with an excuse for Jim on why I was talking with Kate about visiting Barbara Swansey. Perhaps somehow I could lie, cheat, or steal my way out of this horrendous crime.

Chapter Five

Instead, I delayed going out to see Jim and had the perfect excuse—the kitchen faucets.

The aged underground pipes twisted and turned like a large plate of spaghetti, and took ages to get the water to the designated sink. It sputtered for several seconds before flowing into its final destination, and took forever getting hot.

The lack of hot water gave me a delay tactic in facing Jim and his valid charge of insubordination on my part—I had disobeyed his direct order not to get involved with the murder in the village. A man can be taken out of the military, but the military never leaves the man.

So how was *I* going to explain what he'd overheard in my conversation?

Perhaps I could use the "don't know what came over me" technique. *Nah. I've used that too many times in the past.*

Turning from the sink, I leaned my elbows on the kitchen countertop, put my face in the palms of my hands, and allowed my mind to wander back to Dan Swansey.

If his wife, Barbara, didn't kill him, who did?

There were plenty of other potential suspects in the village.

Like Fred and Jessica Trowley. Jim and I were known in the village as "the couples' couple." We had helped several partners with marital issues since Jim had been ordained as a lay minister with the local "free church" when he retired from the military.

The times we'd met with Fred and Jessica had pushed Jim's patience to the limit. Those two were known to get into marital scraps closely resembling a match on World Championship Wrestling. I wouldn't have put it past them to fight while unintentionally killing someone in the process.

One evening last fall, they'd been having a huge argument in the middle of the street as they headed home from the Queen's Treat pub.

+ + +

It was a clear, chilly night. Blustery gusts flipped leaves up and down the lane, and stars seemed to be blue-tacked in space.

Fred and Jessica, oblivious to the attention from everyone in the neighborhood, shared a verbal volley that should have humiliated even them. No one could ignore their yelling even if they wanted to—no one except my Jim. He was propped sideways, asleep in his leather chair.

I threw a purple velour bathrobe over my plaid flannel pajamas and went out in an attempt to stop them from making fools of themselves.

White puffs of brisk air escaped my nose and mouth, and I pulled the bathrobe tighter.

I waved at them as they hissed at each other like two demon-possessed feral cats.

Jessica screamed at Fred, "You're such an eejit."

Even from a distance I could see the blood vessels in Jessica's thick neck bulge and pulsate like water-filled knots in a garden hose.

Fred stretched his tall giraffe neck, his head hanging over her short stature. "I'm an idiot? You're the one who put the cat in the bedroom while we were gone." Fred resembled an evil rendition of Ichabod Crane from *The Legend of Sleepy Hollow*. "Now the wild thing thinks it's *his* room. I've tried every trick I know to get him out of there. And I'm tired of sleeping on the couch because you won't get rid of him."

Jessica perched on her tiptoes, thrusting her face closer. "Well, he's better company in the bedroom than you are."

Fred swung his head back and forth, glancing up and down the street. Lights flicked on, and neighbors stood in shadowy doorways. He growled low, but loud enough for me to hear. "Keep the noise down, Jessica. Everyone's listening."

"I don't care what those fools think." She made her statement around his shoulder and directed it to the public viewers, punching her finger into the air toward them.

Several doors clattered shut.

She faced Fred. "The cat stays in the bedroom. You sleep where you want."

Jessica had six cats at last count, and I knew for a fact there were times she treated them better than she did Fred.

As they moved down the street and turned the corner, their noise escalated to the pitch of a loud, boiling teakettle.

Fred and Jessica were certainly viable suspects for murder in the village, if uncontrolled rage counted for anything.

+ + +

Warm wetness sloshed under my feet, soaking both socks. Water ran over the top of the watering can, spilled over the sink and onto the floor, leaving me with yet another mess to clean up.

I wanted to shut my mind off from thinking about who murdered Dan as firmly as I shut off the tap. But the thoughts continued to swirl.

Did Fred know Dan? Did Dan flirt with Jessica?

Fred definitely had a temper, especially when it came to his wife. His jealousy was renown in the village.

There was the time at the pub when Fred broke another man's nose when the guy merely winked at Jessica.

With determination, I grabbed the long-handled mop and swished the water around the floor and into a bucket.

It was time to face the firing squad and talk to Jim about my conversation with Kate. I had put it off long enough.

I threw back my shoulders, lifted my chin, and headed out the back door with a teapot of surrender, a few McVitie cookies—known in the UK as biscuits—and an apology about my phone call sitting on the tip of my tongue.

Chapter Six

Spitting rain left coin-shaped drops on the pavement.

"I'm sorry, Jim. For thinking about visiting Barbara Swansey after you asked me not to get involved."

Jim focused on filling two hanging baskets and trimming off dead leaves and flower petals. He shrugged and continued to clip and shape the bowls of foliage.

I carried the tray to the small summerhouse in the corner of the garden. The bottom half of my apron flipped sideways in the wind and almost knocked the tray out of my hand.

Swinging chimes from a black-chromed hook clanged together over the doorframe, creating the noise of a crazed xylophone.

Inside the summerhouse were two rattan chairs with flowered cushions and a small table. Many evenings Jim and I sat huddled out there enjoying quiet conversations—Jim being quiet and me making conversation.

I ran back inside the house, grabbed the watering can, and placed it at Jim's feet. "I'm sorry this took so long." I retreated into the summerhouse.

As Jim measured his special fertilizer into the can, the spitting changed and began to pelt large raindrops.

He dashed to the summerhouse. Rain rat-a-tatted on the roof like a tap dancer skipping across metal. We sat in silence as I poured our tea.

The sound finally changed to a softer clickety-clack.

"Dotty." A firm word from Jim said a million. He removed his Yankees baseball cap and wiped his brow with an old piece of recycled T-shirt he used for cleaning. He placed the cap backwards on his head.

"I know."

He sipped his tea. "I don't want anything to happen to you; that's all I've been trying to say."

"I know. But I thought if I could do something to *help* Barbara..."

His gaze above the cup stopped me mid-sentence.

"Okay, you're right. I won't go and visit her."

Choosing my words carefully I continued, "But I was wondering..."

Jim's questioning eyebrow lifted.

"Lillie called and asked if we would attend a town meeting tonight to discuss the murder, and what it means for the community. Would you go with me? We need to at least stay informed of what's going on."

He peered through the summerhouse window. A trellis hung along the fence and water dribbled down the wood frame. Climbing white and red roses would provide additional color and shade in the months ahead.

I almost heard the mechanism of Jim's brain in motion.

I learned long ago not to say anything during the time he needed to mull over a request. Marriage can be like a game of chess—a test of wits on who can wait the longest for the other to make a move.

Jim's crooked smile confirmed his mind was made up. He nodded yes. The glimmer in his eyes also showed me we were back on track with one other. Another marital chess piece moved.

A few more clickety-clacks, and the sun broke through the gray haze.

The summerhouse transformed into a romantic scene from *Sense and Sensibility.* Streams of sunlight illumined specks of dust dancing around us like tiny fairies, and a golden glow penetrated the shelter.

I lifted Jim's cap, kissed him on the head, placed his cap facing forward, picked up the tray, and headed indoors to complete my cleaning.

There's nothing quite like a cup of tea and a biscuit to soothe the savage beast and to complete another round of matrimonial chess.

+ + +

At precisely half past seven we crossed the street and entered the village hall's back door.

I had removed my apron and changed into tan slacks and a lilac-colored sweater. Over my shoulder, I carried an oversized, bright multi-stripe handbag with matching dangling threads.

The Neighborhood Watch meeting was exactly like I knew it would be. Not everyone was there, but certainly the ones I suspected would come did.

Three elderly widows sat in the back left corner of the room nattering.

Vivian, the eldest of the three, was as eccentric as they come. She wore a black-checked overcoat in spite of the warm evening. Her grand bouffant, variously colored over the years, shined deep maroon in the light. Harsh makeup accentuated the crevices in her face. But she was a jewel of a woman and generous to a fault.

Vivian spoke loud enough for everyone to hear. Her hearing aid was probably turned down or completely shut off. "This hall is in dire need of renovation."

Sitting on either side were her companions, Annette and Evelyn.

"I heard they're planning on updating soon," Annette said, as she flung her silver hair back and forth, speaking first to Vivian and then to Evelyn.

Shy Evelyn smiled demurely. They say opposites attract; although these three were inseparable, they were as different as the sun, moon, and stars.

Vivian clapped her hands, nails painted the matching maroon of her hair. "It's about time they do something with this place. The only ones using it is the geriatric crowd." She flung her arms in dramatic action, sweeping the room with a long gesture. "All they do is play bingo, teach two-step, and hold table sales in here. What this place needs is a fresh coat of paint and some bright neon lights." She exaggerated her motions as if she were an actress on center stage.

The other two widows nodded in hearty agreement.

She continued, "They need Wi-Fi, maybe some eclectic furniture, and even an espresso machine. They need to turn it into a place where young people want to come and hang out with their friends."

Who would ever have guessed Vivian knew what Wi-Fi was, never mind espresso?

Annette and Evelyn looked at each other and smiled, confirming their fearless leader's wonderful suggestions.

I waved in their direction and moved further inside the hall.

My nostrils caught the lingering smell of musty old books. Bare light bulbs swung overhead, drawing attention to stale smoke hanging in strips of dingy wallpaper—the perfect setting for a Hitchcock movie.

Reluctantly, I had to admit Vivian was right.

As I took in the dreariness from ceiling to floor, I thought it would take a lot more than paint and new furniture to give it the required overhaul it desperately needed. Something more like a John Deere tractor to level it and start from scratch.

Signs posted on telephone poles throughout the village announced an upcoming renovation for the place. Beginning next week, a new paint job and resurfacing of the driveway would be the first steps.

Fred and Jessica were front and center, snug and cozy like two love birds in a pet shop. Surprise, surprise. Although they constantly fought they were always available for town meetings, ready to give their opinions to everyone else. They looked around from side to side, as if any minute they would jump up and take control of the crowd.

Carl the village window washer, Arty the postman, and Jon the shop owner sat together in the center of the room. If anyone knew what was going on in the village it would be them.

Kate had revealed Arty Smith and Dan Swansey had a fight prior to Dan's death.

I wonder what the fight was about.

Arty had on an oversized tweed cap and was several inches shorter than the man on either side of him. With his small build he appeared more like a jockey than a postman.

Did Arty know Dan before he came to the village? Dan was an American from California and Arty was British, so how would they have met?

Petite, twenty-something Police Constable Jones, otherwise known as Jonesy, was smartly dressed in her official uniform. She stood in the back of the room talking on her cell phone and watching the crowd.

Jonesy nodded in my direction and turned her back, continuing her conversation. "We've no reason to suspect him."

I walked nearer, my ears perked like a hunted bunny. I swung my bag to the opposite shoulder in order to get closer. The dangling threads on the handbag spun and slapped, nearly hitting Jonesy on the backside.

"Dotty?"

Spinning, blushing, and uh-humming all at the same time, I faced Jim. "What?"

"Where are you going?"

"Wanted to say hi to Jonesy."

His raised eyebrow told me he didn't believe a word of it.

"I wanted to find out whether she's been picked up for her promotion to sergeant," I added.

Jim wrapped his arm around my shoulders and guided me toward some chairs he and Kate had reserved in the back, far right side of the room.

"You know perfectly well she has a few months to finish her two-year probationary period before she gets promoted. You are not fooling me for one minute, Dotty Weathervane." The "Dotty Weathervane" was whispered sharply in my ear.

"Okay. I wanted to hear what she was saying. What's wrong with me listening?" I glanced over his shoulder while he gently guided me into the seat.

"It's called eavesdropping." He sat next to me, and Kate followed.

Jonesy shut off her cell and walked past the aisles of folks scrambling for seats. She tucked a loose strand of short, curly black hair around her ear as she swung her cap under her arm, while scanning the room as if looking for someone. She moved up front and stood close to where Lillie Bakersfield, the neighborhood watchdog, sat.

Lillie's husband, Jake, still wearing his mud-clogged farm gear, was propped next to her—they were true "fen folk" right down to their wellies. He and Lillie had lived in East Lark since they were both youngsters, a rare breed these days with the mobilization of families zigzagging across the country.

Lillie partially stood and looked back over everyone's heads, waved, and shouted in our direction. "Yoo-hoo, Dotty. Hi, Jim."

Jim gave her a half-salute, trying to keep a low profile—impossible with Lillie in the room.

Kate, dressed in an elegant cream-colored silk blouse and dark brown suede skirt, leaned over Jim and whispered to me, "Guess you were right when you said you thought this meeting was going to be a Lillie show." She cocked her head toward the front. "Look at her sitting up there acting as if she's in charge."

I leaned across Jim's lap to Kate. "You know how she is. She wants to solve the murder, guaranteeing her face on the front page of the *Daily Mirror*." I giggled, in spite of the building tension in the room.

Kate's expensive perfume wafted around her like a soft cloud. "Dotty, you and I both know Lillie has a bad habit of inserting herself into other people's affairs." She spoke with firsthand knowledge, having experienced Lillie's interference one too many times herself.

Jim glared at me sideways as he shuffled in his seat and crossed his legs and arms.

I leaned behind him to speak further to Kate. "Look at how Lillie's dressed. She should change her name to Miss Marple with the floppy hat and homespun sweater she's got on. She's even trying to look like her."

Whereas Miss Marple was a spinster, Lillie was a wife and mother of three grown sons. Miss Marple was unsuspectingly thrown into various mysteries, whereas Lillie looked intently for anywhere she could plunge headlong into someone else's affairs.

Kate leaned back. Jim's neck caught the whispers between us. She said, "I saw the handle of an enormous kitchen knife and a set of large knitting needles jutting out of her tapestry purse when she came in. I wonder if she thinks she'll knit the killer a sweater."

Jim uncrossed his legs, thrust one arm in front of each of us, forcing us to face front. "Shhh. Please. I'm trying to hear what Walter is saying."

Bam. Bam. Bam. A gavel hit the top of the worn table sitting on the raised platform. "Attention, everyone."

Retired magistrate Walter Reed rarely got to pound the wood anymore so he struck his gavel with fervor, bringing the meeting to order. Walter was rarely seen without a stiffed-necked, starched white Savile Row shirt and bright tie. The comb-over on his sun-spotted, perfectly shaped bowling ball head was getting thinner and thinner.

"Attention. Please." *Bam. Bam. Bam.*

"Get on with it, Walter," Carl the window washer shouted.

"Yeah," several of the other men yelled in unison.

"As everyone's probably heard by now, we've had a murder in East Lark." Walter cleared his throat.

"Tell us something we don't already know," Carl retorted. The others laughed in derision.

Walter's frustration sprang from his neck, rising to his cheeks. His face turned the color of a pomegranate. "Will you please be quiet, Carl?" He exhaled slowly and shook his head, his comb-over flipping to the other side. "As I was saying, there's been a murder in East Lark. And we need to defend ourselves from this serial killer." The last two words were said with a trembling emphasis and a shaking of the gavel, as if Walter was intentionally stirring the pot of emotions in the crowd.

A buzz resembling a swarm of flies stuck in a window screen traveled around the room. Folks sat straighter in their chairs, and emotional electricity sparked from their growing anxiety.

Uh-oh. Here comes the *Dawn of the Dead* frenzy I worried about. Surely these people were smart enough to know one murder did not a serial killer make?

Cross-armed, Police Constable Jones gazed over the crowd sharper than a hawk checking out roadkill. She appeared ready to lunge, if need be, to take over.

Jim whispered out of the side of his mouth, "Why did you say we needed to come to this meeting? It's so hot in here with these people making so much racket, no ventilation and the windows closed."

I shrugged.

Walter's marmalade tie flashed in the glaring light bulb. He smoothed the edge of the tie as it began to curl. "We need to decide how to protect each other and be sure the OAPs are taken care of." OAP meaning "old age pensioner."

Whoever came up with that acronym ought to be shot.

Several hours passed and the whole scenario made me nauseous. The temperature inside had risen, the smell of sweat mixed with stale odors made my head hurt, and my intestines seemed to twist with each bang of the gavel. I pressed fingertips into my temples in tight, circular motions.

Lillie could be annoying, but at last she came up with a solution. Stepping up to the platform, she grabbed Walter's gavel and banged the table with one loud crack.

Ouch, did she really have to do that?

She took her Miss Marple hat off. "Why don't we create a phone chain? We'll put everyone's name in my hat and each draw one name. Neighbors will call each other to be sure each is safe—at least until the killer is found."

Everyone applauded, tired with the longevity of the meeting.

Fred and Jessica stood, raised their arms, and clapped.

Vivian shouted, "Hear, hear." Her maroon nails sparkled like magenta jewels as she waved her hands in the air.

Evelyn patted the knees of her two companions. Carl, Arty, and Jon shouted, "Hoorah." Others joined the chorus of cheers. Everyone was ready to get out of the hall-cum-sauna.

Jonesy flitted up and down the side aisles, making her presence known. Tensions were running high and the last thing she needed was a mad rush to the doors—a stampede of overwrought, hot villagers.

I spoke into Jim's ear, "At this point, anything's a welcomed idea if it's going to bring this meeting to an end." Beads of sweat trickled down his temples; the back of his shirt was sopping wet. "Maybe they'll consider putting in ceiling fans when they redo the hall."

Lillie banged the gavel. "We'll each ring one OAP too. Be sure to let me know who you will be calling."

We wrote our names on slips of paper, threw them in Lillie's oversized hat, and pulled out a name as it made the rounds through the room a second time. Each shouted the name they drew.

Arty pulled our names. We got Lillie and Jake's.

Walter grabbed his gavel back from Lillie. *Bam. Bam.* "This is the official ending to tonight's Neighborhood Watch meeting."

We peeled our sticky bodies off the black plastic chairs, and everyone spilled out into the cool evening.

Several folks milled around, chatting a few minutes before heading home. A single lamppost flicked on, the yellow orb lighting a portion of the parking area. Various bugs immediately circled the globe. It seemed an insect party had been spontaneously declared and the entire class of hexapoda from the neighborhood had been invited.

Jake and Lillie exited last out the door and sauntered up to us.

Lillie said, "Dotty, I'm so glad you and Jim came." Her floppy hat drooped over her eyes. I couldn't tell if she was serious or not. "Folks look up to you and I know they appreciated you coming tonight." She lifted the brim and smiled. "By the way, I like the sweater you're wearing. Lilac is lovely on you and brings out the color of your eyes." She grabbed her husband's arm. "Let's go home, Jake."

"Yes, dear," he replied. They were Jake's two favorite words to Lillie.

My jaw dropped. "Will wonders never cease?"

Jim and I crossed the road to enter our house.

He stood aside as he opened the front door, always the gentleman. "Dotty, I think you tend to be a little too critical of Lillie. You need to give her a chance."

"Maybe, but I think she has something up her sleeve. And only time will tell what she really wants. I've seen Lillie lull folks into a false sense of confidence and then pull the rug out from under them one too many times."

Jim followed me in and closed the heavy door behind him.

Chapter Seven

Life quieted down around the village and at home.

The most exciting thing happening was whole milk being on offer, two for the price of one. I ordered several extra pints from Morris, the tallest, skinniest milkman to ever walk the earth. With a ruddy face from years of bitter early morning air, he made the perfect Father Christmas.

In spite of his droopy red and white suit, the children loved him when he threw wrapped toffees or pick 'n' mix into the crowd from the milk truck decorated with Christmas lights and tinsel. Even the adults became childlike when they saw the red-suited gift-giver toss his wares.

We made our daily phone calls to those whose name we had drawn in the Neighborhood Watch meeting—a constant reminder a murderer was still on the loose.

Several days slid by like rain cascading down a window. I thought less and less about Dan Swansey but wondered periodically about his wife, Barbara, and what she would do now. Was she being treated as a suspect? If she wasn't guilty of the crime, was she required to stay and finish her assignment, or would the military send her back to America?

Jim seemed more relaxed about the whole murder business and spent many an hour giving TLC—tender, loving compost—to his garden bed.

Morning light filtered through the kitchen window, leaving crisscrossed patterns along the floor. Empty eggshells lay open in their eggcups like baby birds waiting to be fed.

Jim sat at the kitchen table savoring his last sip of Earl Grey. Cleaned and shaved, he looked rather dapper in his blue-checked shirt. It brought out the deep azure color in his eyes. Instead of smelling like peat moss and dirt, his aftershave had the sweet combination of mint and musk.

The chaos in the kitchen had been chiseled away again, but I still faced garden implements, and clothing draped on a drying rack. Thus making the room resemble a Chinese Laundromat rather than my desired look of a page from *Southern Living*.

We shared the morning paper, both hidden behind a section of news.

BBC music played softly on a replica Kassel AM/FM vintage radio we'd purchased at a secondhand shop.

I sipped slowly from my Queen Elizabeth mug. The warmth of coffee was as comforting as the sunshine pouring like golden syrup through the window.

The music on the radio transitioned. Elton John sang "Can You Feel the Love Tonight?" catching my attention.

My thoughts switched to Barbara Swansey.

What would it be like having your husband murdered and taken from you so suddenly? *Maybe I should visit her and take a pie. See how she's doing.*

Apple pies were my specialty. There's nothing quite like the smell of sweet apples covered with cinnamon, sugar, and butter wafting through a house. Could be why my apron fit so snugly. Perhaps "an apple a day keeps the doctor away" does not include three scoops of vanilla ice cream piled on top of a slice.

Visiting Barbara would have to be handled very delicately. "Um, Jim?"

The paper fluttered.

"Now don't get upset."

Jim slid the paper down. "Dotty, when you start a conversation like that it naturally makes me think what is about to follow is going to make me upset. Why not try again. I'll pretend you didn't say it, okay?" Up the paper went.

"Um, Jim?"

Down the paper went.

There were times it felt like we were volleying over a table tennis net.

"I was wondering . . ."

"Yes?"

"What harm would there be in going to visit Barbara Swansey and taking her one of my pies?" I sped up. No time given for a marital chess move. "After all, the rest of the villagers whisper and point fingers at her behind her back every time she's in the shop. It's like they think she's G.I. Jane out to annihilate everyone. I mean, really, how would it make you feel?"

"All right. Go. But you must promise me you will not ask her about Dan's murder. Are we agreed?"

"Okay. I promise not to bring up his murder." I didn't promise I wouldn't talk about it if *she* brought it up, though.

Plans to visit Barbara were tucked in my mental calendar when a forceful rap on the back door cracked like a karate chop on a chunk of wood.

Chapter Eight

"Wonder who that can be." Jim sat straighter.

"It's pretty early for someone to be stopping by." I wiped egg yolk from my fingertips on a bunched-up serviette.

Most folks are pretty conventional, never dreaming of stopping by without warning, no matter how close the friendship. It's a social faux pas to visit, call, or intrude on anyone during certain times of the day.

"The kitchen is in such a state. Maybe I shouldn't answer." I scanned the room to see how much I could put into place from the time I got up and made it to the door.

Jim shrugged. "Who cares if it's messy?"

The blurred shape shadowed on the door's mottled glass was a familiar form.

I swung open the door. "Kate. What in the world?"

Kate was everything proper in an English woman. When I'd first met her, my harsh accent and somewhat unconventional ways, next to her meticulousness, made me feel like muddy water glopping next to a clear, flowing river. It took awhile, but I had gotten over our differences.

Kate's normally fastidious hair looked like she hadn't taken time to run a comb through it. She was never seen in public without every hair in place, her clothing immaculate. Kate often wore pleated skirts and silk tops except when horseback riding. This morning her crumpled navy trousers and mottled sweater were mismatched and wrinkled. Her cheeks were beetroot red. She twisted her fingers rapidly like an old-fashioned wringer-washer.

She croaked, "There's been another murder in the village." She wiped her brow with a lace hanky she pulled from the sleeve of her sweater.

Jim dropped his paper onto the table atop the eggshells and buttered toast. "What in the world are you talking about, Kate?"

"Haven't you heard?"

"Sit down and let me pour you some coffee," I offered. "Then you can tell us what's going on."

I took her by the arm and guided her to a chair. The sunlight flickered off her bobbed, light-brown hair, and I resisted the urge to pat down the fine strands sticking out on the top of her head. She would be embarrassed if she discovered they were out of place.

Kate pushed her hanky up her sleeve and encircled her fingers around the hot cup I placed in front of her.

She swallowed several gulps of coffee, then exhaled slowly. "Another body was found in the barley fields near the Kelly farm. Can you believe it? This time it's a woman. Maybe we do have a serial killer among us." Her water-rimmed eyes shuffled from mine to Jim's.

"How did you find out? Is this related to the first murder? What's everyone else saying?" My machine-gun questioning was set again on rapid fire.

Jim touched my arm, then Kate's. His pastor-like voice kicked in. "Who is it this time?"

Kate's eyes cleared, and she spoke more lucidly. "No one knows for sure. All I know is what I heard through the grapevine. Everyone's talking about it at the shop. Lillie's knickers are all in a twist because she wasn't the first to find out." Her giggle was strained.

Kate had taught me many phrases Americans wouldn't use, "knickers in a twist" being one. Last week the quip was "a load of codswallop," translated meant someone talking nonsense. Think we were speaking about Lillie then, too.

Jim surprised us with a sudden declaration. "I'm going outside to check on my plants." He took one more gulp of liquid, left the table, grabbed his tools, and headed for the door.

"What? How in the world can you go outside when there's been another murder?" I was dumfounded by his sudden retreat. "Besides, you have your good clothes on."

He shrugged. "The sun's out. But I see dark clouds rolling in. The plants need to be taken care of. Nice seeing you, Kate. Thanks for coming by and telling us the news."

My voice raised a notch. "Jim Weathervane, how in the world can you think of Japanese an-o-moo-ees at a time like this?"

"It's *a-ne-mo-nes*, Dotty. And it isn't the right time of year for them yet."

"I don't care about the plants."

He nodded toward Kate. "There's nothing we can do about this situation right now. We need to wait and see what the police say."

"How can you NOT want to find out what's going on?"

He grabbed his weed weapons of war and shrugged. "Easy." Out the door he went.

Chapter Nine

Through the window, I watched Jim kneeling in the darkened earth knowing full well this was his way to process the latest news.

Bliiiiing.

"East Lark 58 1808."

"Dotty, this is Lillie."

I covered the mouthpiece and whispered, "Guess who?" to Kate.

"Hello, Lillie. Guess you've heard the news?" I said.

Kate knowingly winked at me, placed her mug in the sink, waved a quick goodbye, and mouthed she would call later in the day.

Lillie continued without inhaling. "Can you believe another murder has happened? Are we becoming Midsomer?" She was referring to the famous television series starring John Nettles. She enjoyed the show so much she watched reruns of the reruns.

"I think that's a bit extreme, Lillie. We don't even know if this woman is from East Lark." I chose my words carefully. I really didn't want to hurt Lillie's feelings. She meant well. At least that's what she told everyone when she listened in on others' conversations, spread rumors, or wrote down plate numbers on cars parked illegally in front of Serenity Beauty Salon on High Street to give to the police.

I could hear Lillie clucking her tongue as if to say she thought I was being quite naïve. With a patient sigh she proclaimed, "Dotty, what does it matter where she's from? She's dead in East Lark, isn't she? Besides, I found out her name is Amy Miser."

"How did you find out? I didn't think anyone knew who she was."

"I was talking with Vivian and Annette at the hair salon. They spoke to Morris. He heard it from—"

"Never mind how you found out." This could take all day. "What do you propose we do, Lillie? Have another Neighborhood Watch meeting?" I bit my tongue as a reminder to watch my words. "Doesn't look like the past gathering did anything to prevent this latest murder."

"I think our best plan is to continue with the phone chain. But I'll also call every name in the East Lark phone book and find out what each person might know." She took another deep breath before continuing, "If I can gather enough information maybe I can help the police figure out what's going on. I'm afraid I won't get another good night's sleep until these murders are solved."

If she could hear my eyeballs rolling they would have sounded like ten-pin bowling. "Okay, Lillie, good luck. I have some errands to do today. I hope you're successful."

"I'll keep you posted." She hung up.

Lillie was having a ball. I, on the other hand, had promised Jim I wouldn't put my nose into this mess, other than visit Barbara with a pie. I was determined to keep my word.

Otherwise, Jim might want to commit a murder of his own and the victim would be me.

Chapter Ten

The best way for me to not get involved was to stay busy.

Several errands listed earlier on the backside of an old electric bill, buried somewhere under Jim's pruning shears and a stack of seed packets, would keep me occupied for quite some time.

When we retired, I had dreamed of pristine kitchen counters, clean cupboards, and lounging in my bathrobe sipping endless cups of coffee while reading Dorothy L. Sayers novels. No such luck.

I dug out the list and scanned the barely legible words I'd written without wearing my reading glasses:

First: Pauline's.

Spinster, teacher, and next-door neighbor, Pauline was away on a two-week vacation to Malta. I offered to water her plants and feed her two overweight felines. We rarely saw Pauline, but the cats periodically visited our front step, leaving gigantic hairballs as a parting gift.

Second: Erika and Jason's, drop off baby gift for Addie.

Tall, sleek Erika never showed when she was pregnant—or as they say across the pond, "had a bun in the oven"—and already had her lean body back. I would never see lean on me again. Come to think of it, lean and me had never met in the first place.

Third: Take pie to Barbara—if she was still around.

After transferring my bits and bobs from the multi-striped handbag to a cream one with various-sized purple spots, I draped the stuffed bag over my shoulder. The poundage pulled on my arm.

Before heading out to do my errands, I needed to let Jim know where I was going. I stood at the window and watched him as he worked in the garden. He had refilled the bird feeders, cleaned the birdbath, and picked up his tools. The whole area looked fabulous.

Think I'll surprise him with a small garden party for a few of our neighbors. Show off all of his hard work.

"Yoo-hoo, Jim." I rapped on the kitchen window.

His back faced the house, but I saw one of his tattered gloves and slightly bent trowel on the ground beside him.

There goes another pair of good trousers being destroyed.

The back of Jim's bald head glistened.

Sigh.

He forgot his cap again. Jim would be a lobster if the sun chose to honor us with its presence. With several sunspots speckling his head, the dermatologist warned him not to expose himself too much to the sun. Usually not a problem in East Lark, but he still had to take precautions.

I stepped outside.

Sparrows darted from suet-ball feeders and perched on overhead branches waiting for me to leave so they could continue their feast.

"Jim, here's your cap. Kate's left. Lillie called to fill me in on what she knew about the woman who was murdered—which was basically nothing other than her name. Amy Miser. Now I'm heading out to do some errands." He didn't respond. I bent over and followed his stare. "What are you looking at?"

His face was buried deep in the hedge. The muscles in his arms were hard at work. He pulled on something, yanked, and collapsed on his backside.

"Jim?"

"Dotty, I think I might have found something."

He gingerly lifted up a long, gruesome-looking knife by the handle. I could see red coloring caked on the tip of the blade.

"Put that thing down," I squealed. "You're leaving your fingerprints all over it. We don't want the police suspecting you of anything."

Of course, suspecting my Jim of hurting anything bigger than a spider was beyond ridiculous.

He spoke slowly and deliberately in spite of the fact that a lethal weapon was dangling from his hand. "Dotty, I put my glove on before I touched it."

I snapped, "Here I was trying *not* to worry about these two murders. And you go and dig up some kind of weapon in our garden."

"What do you think, Dot? I wanted to find this thing?"

"Let's bury it."

"You can't be serious."

"Of course I'm not serious. But you can't blame me if we get more wrapped up in this mess than you wanted us to. This is not my fault."

I stomped my foot and headed inside to call PC Jones. I was sure when she heard the news, she would be over quicker than it took to order Chinese takeaway and the unrequested fortune cookies that came with it.

Chapter Eleven

Jonesy arrived accompanied by a tall, good-looking chief inspector whose black uniform sparkled.

CI Sean O'Reilly was a pureblooded Irishman with cobalt eyes, red wavy hair the color of fall leaves in New England, and a chiseled chin that made him the perfect stand-in for a young Sean Connery.

It had to be a thrilling time for Jonesy. For a young, motivated policewoman, the murders might be just the ticket for promotion to sergeant.

The large knife Jim had found in the garden sat centered on the coffee table. Two spots of dark red blood on the blade's tip resembled menace-filled eyes that seemed to scowl at us.

Chief Inspector O'Reilly asked, "Tell me again, Mr. Weathervane, where you found this."

"In the hedge under some weeds."

The Westminster clock chimed eleven and echoed throughout the house. As the sound faded, quiet discomfort filled the living room. Brief morning sun sneaked behind growing cloud cover, casting dark shadows on the carpet. The entire scenario felt like a scene from *Dial M for Murder*.

Pencil tapping notepaper, O'Reilly cleared his throat. "Mr. Weathervane, we'll have to dig around where you found the knife. Might be something else out there. We'll send a team over this afternoon around half past one. In the meantime, we have to cordon off the area." He jabbed his pencil in the air toward Jim with small sword thrusts.

Jim's shoulders dropped. "Do what you have to do." After so many years of marriage, I knew what he was thinking: his bedding plants would be mauled to death.

Jonesy took the knife by the handle with a small set of forceps and placed it in a thick plastic bag.

O'Reilly slapped the notebook shut and glared at Jim for a long moment. His voice sounded smooth as silk, but his eyes were cold and indiscernible. "I'll be back in touch once my men have a good look around."

I escorted them to the door. "Do either of you know if Captain Swansey is still here, or has she gone back to America? I want to visit her but I'm not sure if she's still around."

PC Jones placed her cap on. Splays of short black curls sprang out at odd angles around her face. Her dark brown eyes betrayed hesitancy. "Barbara Swansey will have to stay here for the time being. She has to finish up some last-minute details with the coroner's office." She and O'Reilly departed.

I straightened the living room and prepared to head out to take care of my to-do list.

Jim stood in the doorway leading to the kitchen, head bowed. "How about going to the pub for lunch? Afterwards I'll help you with your errands."

"*Really?*"

"I don't want to see the police dig up my garden."

I resisted the urge to drop my list, dance around the room, and jump into Jim's arms. Maybe we should find murder weapons in our garden more often if it meant a lunch treat at the pub in the middle of the week.

We strolled to the Hare and Hound. Crisp mornings with frosty dew on the grass made me think spring was trying to wake up without having much success.

"Look at Mr. Giles in his ancient tractor." I waved in his direction. Mr. Giles was nearing ninety with grooves on his face matching the ruts in his field. Seagulls resembled tiny ballerinas in *The Nutcracker* as they frolicked behind his machine amid rows of chunked soil.

He shot us a wave and returned to his task.

The pub was quiet when Jim and I sauntered in. Schools were out for spring break so many families were away on holiday.

The Hare and Hound was somewhat typical of a village pub, although some had more character than others. We'd been to pubs where the original seventeenth-century beams were still exposed and fires burned in inglenook fireplaces used by knights of long ago. Here the tables were adorned with plastic flowers in clear vases, mismatched tablemats, and paper serviettes. The food was superb though. Their fenmen pie was the best I had ever eaten — and I'd eaten a fair share of pies.

Five men sitting on stools at the bar twisted in our direction and nodded to us in sequence.

Fred and Jessica were at one table near the front.

I slid my arm into Jim's and whispered, "Hope they behave and don't get into an argument while we're enjoying our lunch."

Judge Walter Reed sat at another table munching on chips, reading a legal manual, and sipping Strongbow cider, his peony pink tie askew.

"Psst. What do you think?" I whispered to Jim again.

"About what?"

"If Walter would lose about thirty pounds and cut off his comb-over, he might be considered nice-looking."

"Can't say he's my type." Jim gave me a crooked smile.

I elbowed him. "Hey, maybe I could get him and Pauline together. They're both alone and would enjoy each other's company. I'm sure of it."

Jim pulled his arm away.

"We could have them over for dinner and a game of cards. Give them both something exciting in their lives besides fat cats and legal mumbo-jumbo."

I looked around Jim's right shoulder at Walter. His face was still buried in the manual, his jaw working on two chips protruding out of his mouth.

Jim took my face into his hands. "Dotty, I don't like you playing matchmaker any more than I want you getting involved with a murder. It could cause you nothing but trouble."

"Fine."

Jim put his mouth closer to my ear. "Dotty, don't look now."

"Where?"

"I said don't look. Why do you do the opposite?"

"Habit."

"Why do I bother?" He guided me to a nook near the bar counter, away from the larger dining area to a cozy table for two. It was a tight squeeze getting into two worn chairs snuggled under the round faded oak table.

In spite of it being spring, embers burned in the fireplace and dampness lingered.

"What didn't you want me to look at?" I opened a menu that had been propped in a metal holder.

He nodded across the dining area as he grabbed another menu. "At the table in the corner is a group of newspaper reporters and photographers."

I leaned toward him. "Those reporters couldn't know we found the knife in our garden, could they?"

"It won't take long for the news to get out. But let's enjoy our lunch and forget they're here. Okay?"

Jim rose and went the few steps to the bar and gave our drink order to Roger Lacey, owner of the pub. Although I'd heard Roger was from London, he was one of the quietest, most introverted men I knew and I'd had little interaction with him. Roger's short legs were contrary to his long neck and thin arms. Thick bushy hair resembled an oversized toupee atop his head and framed a rather baby-looking face.

"What'll ya have to drink, Jim? It's on me," window washer Carl, sitting on the stool closest to our table, offered.

"J2O for Dot and a shandy for me. Thanks, Carl."

"What'd ya think of these murders?" he asked.

"Not sure what to think. I'm sure the police will figure something out soon."

"Food?" Roger interjected, fingers on the register ready to take Jim's order.

"A fenmen pie for me and a prawn salad for Dot."

Jim carried the drinks to our table and shuffled into his seat across from me.

I sipped the J2O. "You and I haven't had a chance to talk, what with your garden keeping you so busy."

"What do you want to talk about?"

"The murders, of course. What else? Do you think Dan and the dead woman, Amy what's-her-name, knew each other? Do you think he was having an affair and Barbara got wind of it? What did you think about finding the weapon in the hedge? Were you shocked?" I gulped the J2O to replenish my weapon of voice.

Jim patted my hand. "Whoa, Dotty. Slow down. One question at a time."

"Which question do you want first?"

"Don't care." He sipped his shandy and sat back.

I clicked my glass with my fingernails. "Well, what do you think about these two murders? I mean, do you honestly believe we have a serial killer in the village?"

Jim held up his pointing finger. "Only one question, Dot." He popped a garlic-stuffed olive in his mouth from our appetizer trio of olives, homemade bread, and nuts.

"Okay, I slid in two. It's a bad habit I have. You should be used to it by now." I helped myself to a piece of the still-warm bread.

"To answer both your questions, I don't know."

"That's not all you're going to say, is it?"

Jim surprised me by adding, "To quote a famous detective, 'I have no data yet. It's a capital mistake to theorize before one has data.'"

"Detective Barnaby?"

"Nope. Sherlock Holmes." He winked.

There were times Jim was as annoying as an army of ants at a picnic. Other times I couldn't imagine life without him. Especially when he looked so handsome, like he did right then in his gray slacks and the new black-and-gray-striped shirt. We might both be aging but that didn't stop me from thinking he was as cute as Colin Firth from BBC's *Pride and Prejudice*. But come to think of it, Colin Firth looked best without his shirt on as he swam across the pond and exited the water, soaking wet.

Roger placed our meals on the table and left without exchanging a word.

Jim seasoned his food with salt and pepper. "We can consider what we *do* know about the murders so far, Dotty." He took a bite of the steaming fenmen pie that contained chunks of lamb, vegetables, and thick gravy.

I opened my mouth in conjunction with him, and closed it as he savored and swallowed a bite of juicy meat. I'd ordered the prawn salad anticipating a sweet after the main course. My motto: you have to make sacrifices somehow.

"Dan and Barbara Swansey have been here a little over six months, so I can't imagine they know too many people," Jim said.

I poked at my salad.

He forked another piece of meat. "We don't know what Barbara does for the US military, do we?"

"No. She always seemed to avoid talking about it whenever I asked her."

"What do you suppose Dan was doing while Barbara was working on base during the day?"

"Good question, Jim. Not sure." The small prawn perched on the tip of my fork looked rather pathetic next to Jim's chunky bite of beef. "But Kate told me Dan was in a fight with Arty not too long ago." I popped the prawn into my mouth.

"Arty? Did Kate know what the fight was about?"

"Nope."

"Hmm. This fenmen pie is better than the last time I ordered it." Jim took one last bite. "Give me your womanly instinct, Dot. Do you think Barbara Swansey killed her husband?"

"I don't see it. But I was wrong the last time I thought a wife was innocent. What about you? You're a good judge of character. What do you think?"

"I've only met her that one time I went to the shop for a paper, but I'm with you. I don't think Barbara did it either."

Buttering my brown bap—a type of bread roll—I tried not to interrupt Jim's flow of words but couldn't help myself. "So where do you suppose the weapon came from?"

"I've been wondering that too. The only thing I can figure is the murderer threw it across the low-lying wall by the house. I'm sure they wanted to get rid of it as soon as possible when they left the pub and put Dan's body in the dumpster."

"How about this woman they found in the field. Amy Miser? Lillie is trying to help the police. I hope she doesn't get herself into too much trouble."

The questioning eyebrow rose. "Do you *honestly* hope Lillie doesn't get herself into trouble?"

"You know me too well, Jim Weathervane."

We finished our main course and ordered one sticky toffee pudding with creamy custard and two forks.

An hour of uninterrupted, no-garden conversation was wonderful. I wanted it to last forever. Instead, Jim paid the bill and we headed toward the door.

As he opened the door for me, a reporter ran up, blocked our exit, thrust a microphone into Jim's face, and asked a very surprising question.

Chapter Twelve

"Rumor mill has it you found a murder weapon in your garden. Is that true?"

Jim reverted to drill sergeant mode. "Move that thing from my face, young man."

The unshaven, T-shirt-clad twenty-something reporter was undeterred. "Could you please answer the question?" His mike in one hand, a tattered notebook in the other, and a British flag-patched backpack over his shoulder completed the outfit.

A second reporter ran up beside him with a camera. A bright light flashed, and I swung my handbag in front of my face. If I had known we were going to make the headlines, I would have worn something nicer. Perhaps the tutu on the M&S advert page. That would have scared these two reporters to death and we'd be free to leave.

"Sorry, can't answer any questions." Jim pushed the mike aside and guided me out the door.

We walked briskly down Friday Street. I tried to keep up the pace, his stride much longer than mine. "How could they have known about the weapon?"

Jim's jaw was locked and loaded, as he spoke through gritted teeth. "Someone told those reporters."

"But who knew besides Jonesy and Inspector O'Reilly?"

"That's a good question. And it's one I am going to find the answer to, right after we finish your errands."

+ + +

We watered Pauline's plants and fed her fat cat.

Dropped off a baby gift—Paddington Bear with suitcase in hand—for Erika and Jason. Jim wrapped his arms around baby Addie for several minutes and nestled her close.

We said our goodbyes and headed home with Jim whistling. The time with Addie had calmed him, and he was better prepared to confront whoever told the reporters we'd found the knife in our garden.

"Can you believe those guys at the pub?" The front door clicked behind me as we proceeded to the kitchen. "I want nothing more than this mess to be over and get our lives back to normal." My bunions thanked me as I took off my shoes.

"I'm going to make some calls and find out who spoke . . ." Jim paused mid-sentence as he stood at the French-door windows looking out at the garden, motionless as a mannequin.

"What's wrong?"

He pointed. Mounds of black dirt were piled everywhere. It appeared more like an upside down chocolate cake than Jim's flora masterpiece. Plants were strewn along the border. A deep cut in the hedge where the knife was found looked like a madman with a machete had hacked it. Tools sat in a large heap in a corner.

"I'm so sorry, Jim. You've worked so hard."

It's going to be some time before I have a garden party for him now.

He turned around and went upstairs.

Two minutes later he was back down, changed from his "pub-wear" into garden-work attire.

Instead of making calls to find out who snitched to the reporters, it seemed he would rather give CPR—critical plant resuscitation—to bring dead foliage back to life. I knew without a doubt, he'd spend the rest of the day salvaging what was left of his plants and cleaning up the mess.

Chapter Thirteen

The police put a halt to reporters writing anything about the weapon being found for two reasons: to protect us from being harassed and to give the killer confidence that the knife was still hidden. In turn, we were told not to say anything to anyone. Everyone was suspect until more information could be found.

We were happy to agree. But who told the reporters in the first place?

It was still a mystery where the woman in the barley field, Amy Miser, had come from. And no one was remotely considered a suspect in Dan Swansey's death. Were the crimes related? No one knew for sure.

The police had no further questions about the knife in the garden, which they told us was some type of small bowie knife. It turns out that bowie knives were made popular in the early nineteenth century by Colonel James Bowie from Texas. Go figure. A Texas-sized knife in a British-sized garden. No wonder it was so easy to find.

The phone chain no longer worked. Folks were tired of the habitual conversations that mattered little to the issues at hand.

Lillie stopped pestering me. I felt a tad sorry for her since my guess was she was bored with nothing going on with the investigation.

Gone was my desire to visit Barbara. I got back to a quieter East Lark life: reading, listening to BBC Radio Three, and trying my hand at a bit of writing. Several ideas about writing a romance novel ruminated in my brain, and I wanted to jot down some thoughts. Plus, Kate's birthday was coming up and I wanted to treat her at Molly's Tea Leaf. There was plenty to do to keep me busy.

Tuesday morning, I shifted things from my polka-dot handbag to my latest charity shop purchase—a gold filigree, long-handled purse large enough to fit a kitchen sink in.

I had a ten o'clock hair appointment at Serenity with my hairdresser, Fiona.

"Bye, Jim." I poked my head into the living room.

He sat reading a do-it-yourself garden manual, figuring out how to bring life back into the plants molested by the savage investigative team. His brow furrowed as if he were a surgeon operating on a patient.

A quick peek in the front hall mirror confirmed a little lipstick might be in order. Color brushed along my lips and running fingers through my hair made no difference whatsoever, but the attempt made me feel like I was at least making an effort. I needed a redo of my hairdo, and Fiona had always done wonders.

I loved my hairdresser appointments for many reasons, reasons only women understood. Chatter, gossip, and camaraderie were experienced at a hairdresser that never happened elsewhere. Serenity Salon was no different.

One last look in the mirror and I was good to go.

Noise outside caught my attention and I opened the door. Men jumped out of unmarked white vans parked across the street, and unrolled temporary fencing bales and stacks of wood in preparation for the upcoming work on the village hall.

"Guess they're starting to work on the renovation," I shouted back at Jim.

"Huh?"

I went back into the living room. "I said, I guess they're starting to work on the renovation of the village hall," I yelled above the din of the men outside.

His face was still plunged in the plant manual. "That's nice."

I pulled the door closed behind me.

Walking to the salon, I passed posted signs on telephone poles announcing that the work on the hall would last a month. I wondered if Vivian would get her way with an espresso machine and Wi-Fi.

+ + +

Even in a small village like East Lark there was much to enjoy: from gardens to animals, flowers to fruit. There were honey makers and jam sellers. One farmer, Peter, sold reasonably priced vegetables outside his cottage on a man-made wooden stand covered with an ivy-green vinyl shade.

Everything was within easy walking distance, too. Serenity Hair Salon was only two doors down from the village shop and a few blocks from home.

The pear tree in Erika's front garden was bursting with small buds, which would eventually develop into fruit that would drop and feed many a blackbird. Each year she generously gave Jim and me bags of the abundant produce. In turn I would provide pear sauce and crumble for her dinner table. It was a wonderful symbiotic relationship.

I stopped to enjoy several gardens along the way—many the size of postage stamps.

Trumpeting daffodils lifted their brilliant yellow faces skyward, and white and pink blossoms covered various bushes. Creativity could be capitalized upon even in a tiny space, and it seemed every British national I knew had a green thumb. Not me. Black is the color of my thumbprint—I kill any plant within watering distance.

I closed my eyes and inhaled the sweet fragrance.

A car drove past, and I opened one eye.

The red-squared Royal Mail vehicle pulled to a quick stop a few doors down. Arty jumped out. I waved but he didn't notice. He seemed frazzled as he scurried from house to house, pushing mail, magazines, and unsolicited flyers into door slots. As quick as I could say "post" he was back in the vehicle and zipping up the road.

As I continued on to Serenity, a golden retriever lopped by on the other side of the street, his yellow-haired underbelly covered in mud. It was unusual to see a dog not on a lead.

The animal stopped to take care of some business, sauntered up to the bright red door of Number Ten, and barked.

They must be Americans living there.

And most likely unaware of this country's regulations about pets. If the dog were seen without its owner, they would get a stern warning and perhaps even a fine for a thousand pounds.

Someone heard the dog's bark, opened the door, and the retriever waddled inside.

I turned a corner, and my shoe caught on an upturned chunk of cement. *"Ouch."* I leaned down and rubbed my ankle.

A white envelope, what looked like a small piece of mail, lay upside down in the dirt near an azalea bush not yet in full bloom. Arty must've dropped it when he rushed from house to house.

I'll just give it to him when I see him again on his rounds.

The envelope was addressed to Dan Swansey. No return address. No identifiable handwriting. No steam nearby for me to loosen the glue off the back so I could open the thing either. What a shame.

Putting the envelope into my bag, I reached down to rub my foot again. Wedged between the bush and the corner of the building was a piece of some sort of fabric with sparkles.

I tugged at it.

Out came a man's very expensive Italian Forzieri glittering gold and red necktie, its special logo sewn on the inside. *Break* had an article not too long ago on the resurgence of men wearing ties and had highlighted this particular brand. Attached to each end of the tie was a lady's stocking leg.

The morning paper said Amy Miser had been strangled. Postmortem results indicated the markings on her neck came from nylon of some sort. Surely this wasn't the thing the killer used?

I glanced around and pushed the tie with the nylons into my handbag. Somehow I felt like a child caught with her hand in the cookie jar. But this was no cookie and I was no child.

How was it Jim and I both found something potentially connected to these crimes?

Maybe I could stick these things back under the bush, call Lillie, and tell her to come and dig them out. She'd love to be in the middle of an investigation, put on her floppy Miss Marple hat, and give the police her opinion as to the identity of the murderer.

"That's not a good idea either." She'd wonder how I knew the stuff was under there and wouldn't let me rest until she pried a confession from me. My imagination took off and I could see bright lights glaring in my eyes, water torture, or bamboo shoots under my fingernails as potential options for Lillie's use in prying out what I knew.

I cringed. My hair appointment would have to wait.

Zipping up my purse, I scurried back home, unable to enjoy the colorful flowers or romantic aura along the way.

Cumulonimbus clouds formed in the distance, perhaps a bad omen of what lay ahead for the rest of my day.

Chapter Fourteen

Rain started to patter on the windows as soon as I stepped into the house.

With a huge heave, I threw my purse on the kitchen counter.

I pulled out the tie with nylons, piled it on top of the bag, and called PC Jones before telling Jim. There was no point in getting him worked up sooner than necessary.

"This is Dotty Weathervane. I'd like to speak to Police Constable Jones, please. It's a matter of urgency."

As I waited for Jonesy to come on the phone I emptied some of the miscellaneous things out of my bag. Hair clips, shop receipts, golf ball found in the front garden. Where did all this stuff come from? Hadn't I just changed bags? And how in the world did a golf ball end up in our garden? Stuff shuffled and shook.

"Mrs. Weathervane. How nice."

I stopped my purse cleaning.

Jonesy continued, "I was going to call you today and ask you to please go and visit Barbara Swansey. Just a neighborly visit, you understand."

I didn't have a very good feeling about where this is going.

Jonesy placed her hand over the phone's mouthpiece and spoke to someone in her office. She came back on the phone, her voice lowered. "Sorry about that, Mrs. Weathervane. Where was I? Oh, yes. I saw Barbara yesterday and, well, she seemed somewhat in a dither. Of course it's no wonder she's jumpy, the way everyone acts around her in the village.

"Barbara's eyes kept flitting around when I spoke to her, as if she was worried about something. But she said nothing was wrong when I asked. I thought, since you're the one person in the village who doesn't seem bothered by her, maybe it'd be nice for you to stop by with one of your delicious pies and see how she's doing."

No, no, no, was what I wanted to say. I wanted to visit Barbara but on my terms and with my objectives.

Instead I said, "I'd be happy to."

I had a sneaking suspicion Jonesy did not want me to merely pay Barbara a visit. I bet she wanted me to do some investigating to make her look good for that attractive Chief Inspector Sean O'Reilly.

She batted her eyes at O'Reilly with a Cinderella-meets-Prince-Charming-flickering-eyelash glance whenever I saw them together.

Jonesy said, "Just see if she needs to talk. Be a listening ear. You and Jim are both good at that." A little buttering up was going on here and not on a bread roll. "I was wondering while you were visiting if you could poke around a bit too?"

I knew it.

"What do you want me to be poking around for?"

"Prod a little. You know, about her background and her relationship with her husband. Keep your eyes open when you're in her house. Mind you, I'm not saying to break the law or anything."

What was she telling me to do if not to break the law?

"I'll see what I can do. I wanted to visit her anyway. But things seem to keep coming up. Speaking of coming up, I had called to tell you I think the other murder weapon has turned up."

"What? Why didn't you say so?"

Could it be because you didn't give me a chance to say anything while you were talking about breaking the law? I wanted to say. "I found a man's necktie with nylons tied on both ends while walking to Serenity for my hair appointment. What do you want me to do with it?"

"Hang on to it. I'll let the chief inspector know. I'm sure he'll want to come over." She hung up.

In the meantime, I broke the news to Jim. He had the same inclination I had about the knife. Bury it. But of course we both knew better.

+ + +

Chief Inspector O'Reilly and PC Jones arrived fifteen minutes later. They shook their caps to rid them of rainwater and stepped inside. I handed the tie, secured in a plastic bag, over to O'Reilly. We spoke briefly; he asked a few questions and headed to the door.

Constable Jones hung back and whispered, "Now don't forget to be neighborly to Barbara, okay?"

"Constable?" O'Reilly spoke harshly as he stood by the open door waiting for Jonesy.

Out they went.

"What did Constable Jones mean by that remark?" Jim asked.

"She wants me to go and visit Barbara."

"Oh." He went back to his leather chair and do-it-yourself plant book and continued digging for answers on salvation for seedlings.

After canceling my hair appointment, removing a pie from the freezer, and putting it in the oven, I gave Barbara a ring.

When there was no answer, I left a message on her answering machine. "Barbara, this is Dotty Weathervane. I'd like to come over for a visit if you're up to it. When it's convenient for you, of course. Please call me back on 58 1808. I look forward to hearing from you."

At least I could tell Jonesy I tried and failed.

Chapter Fifteen

The day was almost over and it was soon dinnertime.

No haircut, no word from Barbara Swansey, and even fewer words from Jim. He had gone outside soon after Jonesy and O'Reilly left. A negative shaking of his head was a good indicator that he still hadn't found any answers in his plant book.

Finding the necktie with nylons under the bush was first and foremost in my thoughts as I cleaned the kitchen, mopped the floor from muddy footprints, and prepared our meal. I shivered at the idea that a killer had handled the tie, and I took two aspirins to stem a throbbing headache.

Constable Jones mentioned that Barbara was home, yet there wasn't any answer when I called. Perhaps she had responsibilities at the base and was working late.

"What's for supper?" Jim stood dripping from head to toe in the mudroom off the kitchen.

His cap drooped over his forehead, dropping large splats of water the size of fifty-pence coins. Mud sloshed onto the small rug as he rubbed his green wellies—aka Wellingtons—against its wool fibers.

Jim knew the exact time to come and get ready for dinner. Every evening at sunset we heard a gravelly rendition of "God Save the Queen" followed by the American national anthem coming from the other side of the airbase fence through an aging speaker system. The patriotic tradition of music on American military bases was not a jab at our colonial separation from Great Britain, just a sentimental custom I rather liked.

Like Pavlov's dog, Jim was ready to eat when the national anthem played. He probably could smell the apple pie for Barbara in the oven, too, and would be disappointed when he discovered it wasn't for him.

I wiped my hands across my apron. "Jim Weathervane, don't you dare come into my kitchen soaking wet. I just finished mopping the floor. Dinner will be ready soon."

"Oh, Dotty, it's only a little water. Besides, you'll be happy to know I saved most of the plants." He grinned as if he had discovered the cure for the common cold, shook his torso, and flung water this way and that like a dog shaking his fur.

The saying goes, "If Mommy ain't happy, ain't nobody happy." But in our house it was more, "If plants ain't happy, ain't nobody happy."

"I'm glad to hear it. But please leave the wet mess outside."

"Yes, dear." He imitated Jake Bakersfield's sing-song response to Lillie.

"After dinner would you mind walking over to Barbara's with me? I'm a bit worried. I tried calling earlier and haven't heard anything back. Jonesy said she was still here."

"Okay." The one-word, wet bandit had struck again.

Jim stripped down to his skivvies and dragged himself up the stairs to wash mud off his arms and face.

Thirty minutes later he came back down, scrubbed clean. A little bit of shaving cream clung to the inside of his right ear.

The phone rang just as we were about to eat our bangers and mash; otherwise known as sausages and mashed potatoes. These particular sausages, made with wood sage and herbs, were my favorite choice from the local butcher—a shop named The Meat Joint.

"Should I answer?" I asked, sausage on a serving spoon going from the pot to my plate.

"Why?" Jim scooped himself a portion of mash, and white steam rose from the emptied spot. "It's probably another one of those unwanted solicitors calling about car insurance, timeshares, or conservatory windows. And I don't want any of those things."

"I'm worried it could be Barbara." I laid down the spoon and picked up the phone. "East Lark, 58 1808."

"Dotty, how are you?"

"Oh, hi, Kate. Sorry you haven't heard from me in a while. We've been busy with some important stuff that's come up." I didn't add . . . things like knives in the garden and a necktie under a bush.

I promised I wouldn't say a word to anyone, including my best friend, in exchange for the newspaper holding back on printing our names.

"I'm just checking up on you. And wondered if you've heard any more news about the woman in the barley field? I couldn't call Lillie and ask her. I would never get off the phone. And I haven't seen a thing in the papers either. I find it rather odd, don't you? I mean, it has been over two weeks since Dan was killed and that woman found."

"Can't say I've heard anything, Kate."

I wasn't really lying. I hadn't *heard* anything. But I *saw* more than I wanted to.

"Jim and I are going to try and visit Barbara tonight to see how she's doing. I'll let you know how it goes."

"Thanks, Dotty. I'll speak with you tomorrow."

The dinner dishes were washed and put away, our umbrellas stood at attention at the back door waiting to be used, and the piping hot pie was snug in its carrier.

We put on our raingear and trotted off. The rain had subsided so our excursion wasn't too dismal, although we had to dodge a few puddles, stand aside for a car that splashed water along our legs, and step into mud clumps periodically—each to be expected on a cool British evening.

Chapter Sixteen

Jim used a flashlight to direct our steps toward Willow's End, Barbara's small, darkened cottage. At one time, weeping willows were lined down the lane and stopped a few yards before the house. The trees were long gone but the name still stuck.

"There doesn't seem to be anyone around." Jim swung the light back and forth across the front of the house.

I stepped to the front door, rapped, and yelled at him over my shoulder. "Let's peek in the windows, see if anyone's inside."

"Shhh." Jim pressed a finger to his lips.

"What are you whispering for?"

"Maybe Barbara's asleep. We don't want to scare her."

We circled the house looking for a window not covered by a drape. For someone trying not to get involved in murder or mayhem, I wasn't doing a very good job of it. So far Jim had discovered evidence in the garden, I found a tie under a bush, I was asked to snoop for the police, and I was now a peeping Tom.

Rubbing the misted glass on a windowpane, I stood on tiptoe to view the dimly lit kitchen.

One counter was covered with pans, dishes, and Pampered Chef stoneware. Stacks of papers stood in piles. A computer with its lid open had multi-colored circles dancing across the screen. Empty food wrappers, cartons, and books covered another counter.

"I don't feel so bad," I whispered. "Doesn't look like Barbara's much of a housekeeper either. Maybe it's a New York thing."

Jim stepped next to me and peered in. "Look! Down there!"

Barbara was lying in a corner on the linoleum floor. Her blond hair was splayed out in a soft semi-circle that caught the computer's light. She lay perfectly still as if she were Sleeping Beauty waiting to be awakened with a lover's kiss.

"Quick, open the door," I screamed.

"Dotty, calm down. It won't do any good getting hysterical."

"How can you remain so calm, Jim? Our village is becoming the *Dawn of the Dead*."

"You're starting to sound like Lillie."

"Now that's unfair." Jim and I would have to talk about this later when we were both a bit calmer. One should never insult someone in the middle of a desperate situation when there wasn't an opportunity to slug him or her with a frying pan.

Jim spun the knob and yanked open the door. "Open the windows back and front. We need to get some air in here. Smells like the pilot light went off."

There were times I didn't appreciate Jim telling me what to do, but this was not one of them. I obeyed like a soldier to a commander in battle. Within minutes the house filled with a cross breeze of cool air.

Jim cradled Barbara's head in his hands and took her pulse.

I sniffled. "This is dreadful."

"She's unconscious, but I think she'll be all right."

While Jim monitored Barbara I called 999—emergency services in the UK—and PC Jones's cell phone. She had given me the number in case I learned anything from visiting Barbara. All the while my hand shook as if I had eaten a gallon of chocolate espresso beans.

Within minutes I heard the ambulance and stepped outside. Sirens blared and flashing red lights created eerie shadows along the lane.

Water splashed out from under both sides as the vehicle hit deep ruts and bounced. Right behind the ambulance came two police cars, Chief Inspector Sean O'Reilly in the first, Jonesy in the second.

I signaled to them like a ramp attendant directing a plane to its gate and went back inside.

"I'm fine, really." Barbara had regained consciousness and leaned against Jim.

Jim rubbed her hand. "I'm sure you are. But you need to let the doctor check you."

"Poor thing, I feel so sorry for you." As they placed Barbara on the stretcher I touched her cold shoulder.

Although her breathing was steady and her color was returning, she looked weak and helpless.

They wheeled and lifted her up into the back of the yellow-checked ambulance.

"I'll come and see you again when they've decided you're okay to come home," I said.

She mumbled through her oxygen mask, "Thank you."

They closed the back of the vehicle and took off.

O'Reilly and Constable Jones entered the house. She with a pad in her hand and cap snug under her left arm, he with a scowl.

"You two sure seem to find trouble wherever you go these days," Jonesy jokingly remarked. "We should follow you around. Maybe we would solve these crimes in no time at all."

O'Reilly glared at her. She cringed and drew her head into the neck of her uniform.

We settled into Barbara's living room, and Jim and I found ourselves once again fielding questions.

Even though the kitchen was in an upheaval, the rest of the house was neat and tidy. Barbara had taken time to give her home a woman's touch, although some military paraphernalia was in sight.

In one corner sat a large fern; another pot held a yucca plant. Bright splashes of color in modern art hung on the walls, and touristy-type books sat on an oversized mahogany coffee table.

It seemed the Swanseys were planning on visiting National Trust properties before Dan's death. Brochures about Ickworth

House and Anglesey Abbey were also on the table, dog-eared and well perused.

Jim and I sat together in a checked-patterned settee while O'Reilly occupied the overstuffed complementary chair.

Jonesy stood rim-rod behind him, staring straight ahead.

"What happened here? How is it you two are always around when something comes up about these crimes?" O'Reilly's demeanor resembled the frigid winters around New York's Lake Placid. Surely he couldn't think Jim and I had anything to do with this?

I cleared my throat. "Jim and I decided to pay Barbara a visit. I heard she was still in the village and thought she would appreciate seeing a friend." I looked at Jonesy.

She continued to stare straight ahead.

Traitor.

"I called her this morning to see if we could stop by and what time might be convenient. I left a message, but didn't hear back. So I became worried. We came over to check on her and to drop off one of my pies." My words ended up spewing out as if I were shooting watermelon seeds.

Jim patted my hand and took over. "We decided to walk around the house and see if any lights were on or if anyone was home." Jim might be the silent, rumpled type but he always came through for me when I needed him most.

"And what did you see?" O'Reilly growled.

I sat straighter and tightened my jaw muscles.

Jim patted my hand once more, knowing full well I was losing patience with this chisel-chinned god of a police officer. "When we peeked in the window, the kitchen seemed to be in a bit of a disarray. That's when we saw Barbara on the floor. The door was unlocked and it didn't look like anyone had broken in."

"Anything else?"

"Well, there is one thing." Jim made a large arc with his hand. "Doesn't it seem odd there aren't any pictures of Dan and her, anywhere? If you think about it, newlyweds tend to have photos sitting or hanging in their living rooms like proud plaques, don't they?"

Even with Jim and me helping other couples in their marriages, I hadn't thought about wedding pictures. My mind was on murder, not romance. "Good point, Jim. Surely a newly married couple would have some type of wedding picture in their house." Typical British homes don't display marriage photos with the same candor Americans do. "There's no wedding album, photos, or letters anywhere. What do you think it means?"

"I wonder if she could've packed them up since the murder," Jonesy said.

The chief inspector glared back at her. She tucked her chin further into her uniform.

Jim said, "That would be odd too, don't you think?"

O'Reilly tapped his pad with the pencil. "More is going on here than meets the eye."

A few more questions, and the chief inspector and PC Jones left, but not before the windows and doors were closed and locked.

The two police cars pulled out and their red taillights dimmed in the distance.

I flicked on the flashlight. "The chief inspector talked to Jonesy like she was a kindergartener at her first day of class. She seemed a little put out. Wonder what it means for her promotion?"

"Not sure."

"I'm so glad Barbara will be okay. This village couldn't handle having another dead body being found. Think of what it would do. No one would ever leave their homes, or stand around the shop and swap stories. Everything would close: the pubs, the churches, the veggie stand. It would be dreadful."

"Yep."

"Do you think Barbara's fainting was an accident? Do you think someone tried to hurt her? I wonder how this happened. Wonder what I can do to help her when she gets out of the hospital."

No response.

I stopped my nervous chatter.

Even with the small light, the lane was creepy as we walked back home in dead silence.

Neither of us paid much attention to the mud-filled ruts, each of us lost in our own thoughts.

Would life ever get back to being delightfully boring here again?

With two murders, two weapons, and Barbara Swansey in the hospital, I doubted we would see the likes of the mundane for quite some time.

Chapter Seventeen

I pulled the kitchen curtains aside.

Spider webs dangled outside opposite corners of the French kitchen window and glistened in the morning sun. Droplets from last night's rain clung to the intricate design, making them appear like two crocheted doilies.

Moss, washed from the roof overhang, lay in hairy chunks on the pavement, perfect nesting material for birds.

Warm sunlight caressed my entire body. I stood on tiptoe, stretched my arms up as high as they would go, bent at the waist, and touched down almost to the floor.

My exercise regime for the day was complete.

After arriving home the previous night from finding Barbara Swansey on her kitchen floor, I'd put my restless energy to good use. I went through the mess in our kitchen with the speed of a Tasmanian devil. Gone were dirty dishes, stacks of mail, hanging clothes, tools, and recycling bags. White fairy dust was swept away. Even the pine tabletop in the center of the room was naked of clutter.

I slapped my palms together, skipped to the front door, realized my bunion still ached, and slowed to a stroll.

A special offer to have the local paper delivered to our house at half price was one I could not pass up. For the next month the local delivery boy would slide the news through the mail slot, and I wouldn't have to change out of my nightclothes to walk to the shop to buy it.

I felt quite spoiled bending down to pick up the paper. An added bonus was one more toe-touching exercise.

Jim would soon be bounding downstairs, scavenging for breakfast.

Slinging the unopened paper on the table, I began preparing our morning meal, humming "The Sound of Silence."

DYING TO EAT AT THE PUB

"Jim?" I shouted.

"Coming."

Down the stairs he clomped, dressed in his faded green shirt and rumpled trousers. With the sun out, a day in the garden was in store for him.

"Toast and tea? Or do you want some eggs?"

"T and T is fine." Down he went on his chair. Paper opened.

Ah, sweet routine. I have missed you.

Up he flew. "Oh my goodness!"

"What's wrong?"

"Have you seen the headlines?" He sat down again. "You're not going to believe this."

"What? Read it to me. I can't find my glasses." With the mess picked up and everything put away I couldn't find a thing.

Jim read:

"Killer Confesses. Fred Trowley of Potshead Lane confessed to killing Amy Miser, the woman found in the barley field next to East Lark village. He is being held for further questioning in the murder of Dan Swansey. No bail is pending."

"That's impossible." I pulled part of the paper from him and squinted.

My brows were soon going to resemble the furrows in old Mr. Giles's potato fields. "Fred's strange, but he's no killer. What in the world is going on? Do you think Fred could have done this? I mean, why would he do such a thing? Could he have killed Dan, too?"

"It's obvious you're upset, Dotty, but please slow down."

"Do you think Fred is the serial killer?"

"I don't know."

"Guess we can't be sure of anything about anyone anymore. But why would he kill this woman? Knowing Fred's nature, I cannot come to terms with him committing these crimes." I spoke more to the paper than to Jim.

"I'm with you, Dotty. Fred doesn't seem the type."

I jumped up and tossed the paper. Sheets went flying. "I have to go and visit Jessica and see what she has to say. Somehow I can't believe Fred did this."

"Dotty."

I grabbed toast and plates. "Let alone him being with another woman. He doesn't have the charisma to attract a cat, never mind having a mistress."

"Dotty."

I flung them in front of Jim, flipping the plate on top of the toast. "As many times as we met together with Jessica and Fred to help their marriage through some nitpicking nonsense, I always thought Fred loved his wife very much."

"Dotty."

"Fred was definitely tolerant considering the way she treated him."

"Dotty."

"For heaven's sakes, Jim, what?"

"You're a good woman. Please try not to let yourself get so worked up over this. Visiting Jessica is a good idea, but be careful. Remember, I don't want you getting in too deep in this mess. I don't want anything to happen to you, that's all." Those blue eyes gazed up at me with tenderness.

They said I had to love this rumpled, green-shirted fella forever when I declared "I do" those many years ago, and right this minute I knew "I did" with my whole heart.

Chapter Eighteen

Our phone rang at least twenty times before I washed, changed clothes, and headed out the door.

The headline news of Fred Trowley flashed around the village like matches touching dry straw.

Since Jim and I had counseled Fred and Jessica in the past, everyone assumed we knew the history behind Fred and "the other woman." Even the reporters got wind we knew Fred.

Fred confessing to murder was worse than us finding two murder weapons. How did all of this happen? We were knee-deep in the very things Jim wanted us to stay out of: murder, marital infidelity, and mischief. None of which was our own making.

The phone rang again, and I took a deep breath before answering.

Lillie spit through the line. "Dotty, I wanted to let you know they've arrested Fred. They think he's committed both murders." I could almost feel her breathless spray watering my face.

Inhale. Exhale. *Think before speaking.* "Thanks for letting me know, Lillie. I just saw the headlines. I'm going to visit Jessica as soon as I can get ready. I'm sure she's pretty distraught right now. Thanks for calling."

Before Lillie said any more I hung up.

I changed out of my elastic waist pajamas into tightening black slacks and an oversized tangerine-colored top and took a quick look in the front hall mirror before heading out the door.

Tucked in the back of my brain's computer was a reminder to reschedule my hair appointment—that was, *if* I could remember what I was trying to retrieve when the time came to access my mental terminal.

Until then I was off, at a hare's pace, to see what I could do to help Jessica Trowley.

+ + +

Fred and Jessica had a lot of issues. Like the time she locked him in the garage for two days and wouldn't let him out, tossing food and water to him every so often so he wouldn't die. She was mad at him for not taking the trash bin out on the right day for pickup.

I rushed up the street, my feet screaming at the activity.

Across the field a horse handler walked his black-and-white-spotted animal with a red tethered lead, teaching him to canter and trot. On an ordinary day, I would stop and watch the performance. This was no ordinary day.

Fred confessing to murder is wrong. I just know it.

Fred was the epitome of passivity. How in the world could he have killed a woman with a necktie and nylons?

He and Jessica certainly had their troubles. Besides locking him in the garage for two days, there was the time she fed him dog food when he made an off-handed remark about her cooking.

Not merely passive, Fred was downright lazy. As far as anyone knew he hadn't worked in years. He complained of phantom aches and pains, spent many a day in the queue at the medical clinic, and often hung around the front of the Queen's Treat with a cigarette in hand.

Even though he was lazy, he was not an angry bloke. If anyone else's wife did the things Jessica did, they would have kicked her out of the house a long time ago.

Thoughts circled around my mind like the gigantic Ferris wheel at the summer carnival, making my legs move faster—a grand feat, or would that be feet, in itself.

I bent at the knees, put my head down, hands on thighs, and stayed at Jessica's front door for a minute, inhaling deeply. Could it be my morning exercise regimen wasn't quite enough?

After catching my breath, I knocked.

Jessica had obviously been crying, and her wrinkled cream blouse was half-tucked into crumpled khaki trousers, a testimony to many days of wear. Her mascara and makeup melted down her face. With her clothes and face in such a state, she resembled a Chinese Shar-Pei, a rare wrinkled breed known also as the Chinese Fighting Dog—a rather appropriate comparison.

"Jessica, may I please come in?"

She moved aside for me to enter, without saying a word.

I wrapped my arm around her shoulders and guided her back into the house. Three cats scampered this way and that.

"Oh, Dotty, what am I going to do?" She flung herself into my arms and cried without constraint.

I unwrapped her stocky arms, repelled by the repugnant odor caused by her ineffective deodorant. "Let me fix us a cup of tea and we'll sit down so you can tell me what's happened."

Barbara Swansey's home was decorated with artful touches. Jessica's, however, hadn't been cleaned in a millennium. The furniture was dingy and dusty, and the floor unswept. Used cat litter odor seemed to be the air freshener of choice.

Pushing aside some clothes on the sofa, I settled her into the chaotic area she called a living room. "Sit here. I'll fix us a cuppa."

Shock took over. Jessica sat perched on the edge of the couch and stared straight ahead.

A cup of tea soothed the savage beast, but was also good for a lot of other things. *Break* magazine said British nutritionists boasted additional health benefits from tea, including preventing heart attacks. Jessica might be upset but at least she wouldn't have a stroke in the process.

After I poured our drinks, she relaxed somewhat. "Fred and I had a figh' on Tuesday night." Extreme Suffolk accents caused "t's" to drop from some words. Jessica's anxiety accentuated the loss.

She looked at me as if what she said should take me by surprise. It did not.

Cat number four jumped on my lap from nowhere and began to knead my thighs. Not that I disliked cats but I was in no mood to be covered in short ginger-colored hairs or to give the animal its due attention. I placed him on the floor.

Jessica whimpered, "Wednesday morning he told me he was going to the station to speak to one of the police officers. I didn' think anything about it. Thought he was looking for a job."

A job? I tried not to snicker. After all, this was serious business.

She continued, "I was still upset with him so I didn' care where he went as long as he left the house. Now ... he's ... gone ... forever." Each word sputtered between sobs, her heaving chest sending out body odor with each move.

"There, there, Jessica. I cannot imagine Fred doing what he told the police he did. Do you know if he even knew this woman, Amy Miser?"

"I, I, I, I don' know."

"Why do you think Fred would confess to murder? You don't think he could have done this, do you?" Normally I dared not ask her a question about Fred's integrity. She was always difficult with the man, but she defended him like an elephant protecting its young.

Maybe this situation would make her realize she loved Fred, and she'd start treating him like a human being.

She wiped her face on the sleeve of her blouse, leaving mascara streaks along the fabric. "Fred wouldn't hurt a fly. Tha's why I couldn't believe it when they called to say he confessed. Why would he wanna go and do something stupid like that? Doesn't the eejit know I love him and need him?" The last two sentences were spoken with her usual forcefulness.

Jessica confirmed what I already knew. Fred could not have killed the woman in the field. But why did he confess? I had a hunch on that, too.

"Let me see what Jim and I can find out and I'll get back to you. Will you be okay on your own?"

She nodded and stared into her teacup. A long, drawn-out sigh shifted her shoulders up and down like a child who had lost her favorite toy. For the first time, I felt very sorry for this sad, pitiful woman as I left and headed back home.

Chapter Nineteen

"Dot, you had a few phone calls while you were at Jessica's." Jim knelt in the backyard's black soil, adoring pansy faces looking up at him. He was their hero for rescuing them from police infestation and abuse.

"Who called?"

"Kate. She wants you to call her back."

It seemed like ages ago when I last saw her. I missed my times with Kate at Molly's Tea Leaf. We tried to go at least every other week as unpaid quality control experts to make sure the restaurant kept up its standards of scones and teacakes. Someone had to do it. I was willing to sacrifice myself on the altar of indulgence anytime.

"Also, don't forget you've got to see the doctor today at two o'clock."

"Oops. I forgot about that appointment."

He sat back on his calves. "How did it go with Jessica?" His knees dug further into the dirt.

"I told her we would see what we could find out about Fred."

"Is that the royal 'we'?"

"Would you mind calling the police station?"

The questioning eyebrow went up. "What can *I* ask them?"

"I don't know. I didn't know what else to say to her. She was so upset. It was the only thing that calmed her down. She and Fred trust you."

"Fine."

Down went his face, back to his adoring, flowering fans.

Going inside, I glanced around the kitchen. The rotten magician with his mess-making wand was at it again. Paper was tossed everywhere. Wonder who did that? Dishes back in the sink, teakettle and teabags not put away, and other stuff glaring at me with evil glee. It would have to wait.

+++

Lunchtime came and went. Jim ate and went back to kneeling at the altar of the plant goddesses.

I rang Jessica to check up on her.

"Dotty, thanks for coming by this morning." Jessica sniffled.

"Glad to do it. I'll call you later after I take care of a few things." We chatted a few more minutes and hung up. There was hope for the world when someone as hardheaded as Jessica Trowley could thank someone for something.

I hurried to get to the village hall in time for my 2:00 appointment.

Once a week, a doctor—although one always referred to a British doctor as a Mister—attended patients in the village hall. This helped the old age pensioners who didn't drive and kept the waiting time at the main clinic to a minimum. Although the hall was undergoing renovation, they designated a corner for the doctor to continue checking his patients.

Before heading out the door, I changed clothes and threw a few things into another handbag. The one with bright neon green and brown trim I'd purchased at Marks and Spencer's spring sale was just the thing for a bright, sunny day.

Now where are my sunglasses?

Couldn't figure out which was worse: a clean house with no idea where anything was, or a cluttered life and everything right where I left it.

I made a quick visit to the front hall mirror.

That's what I forgot. Make a hair appointment. It would have to wait.

Out I went, new tote in hand.

Why was it whenever I visited a GP—or any other medical professional—and they couldn't figure out why something wasn't working on my body the way it used to, they ended their session with a wink and a nod, saying, "What do you expect at your age?"

I guess I still expected to be able to move, hear, see, walk, and talk, along with having a good night's sleep. But the older I got, the less sleep I seemed to get; thus a visit to the clinic.

A temporary wall had been erected that separated half the inside of the village hall from the other. Muffled hammer tapping could be heard from the other side.

Ceiling and wall fixtures were gone. The old wallpaper had been stripped off, and an undercoat of white paint applied. Light filtered through cleaned windows.

Vivian, Evelyn, and Annette sat in the same chairs they were in during the Neighborhood Watch meeting. This time Vivian was dressed in a knee-length tweed skirt and buttoned up beige cardigan.

"What do you think about the changes to the hall, Vivian?" I settled in the black plastic chair next to her. The other two women nodded and smiled.

"Don't you think a bit of color would do well in here, Dotty?" Her large gestures, with brilliant red nails, almost hit me. "They should paint the walls bright colors. Maybe hang up some impressionistic art."

"I think both of those ideas are great. You should tell the W.I."

"The Women's Institute doesn't want my opinion, believe me." Her wrinkled skin spread upwards with a Cheshire cat grin. "I get up their noses with my suggestions." She leaned in. "I love it when I get those old gals' goat feathers ruffled."

One by one we were called back to see the doctor behind the short privacy screen set up a few feet away. I could hear everything each person said. So much for my hearing being gone "at my age," and privacy being kept for the others.

I was the last to be called in. Mr. Carlton was one of three doctors on rotation to see patients at the hall. The lines around his mouth were so embedded they looked fake—as if they were joined together with nuts and bolts.

He did the usual routine. Throat. Check. Ears. Check. Nose. Check. Sure glad I wasn't missing any of those vital organs. Why he bothered to check them when what I needed was something to help me sleep was beyond me.

"Mrs. Weathervane, you seem to be fine, but I'm going to give you some tablets to help you rest better at night." Smile. Nod. Wink. "After all, these things happen when you get to be a certain age."

Grrrr. I wanted to slug him with my new cheerful, sunny tote.

+ + +

The rest of the day went by like the swallows that swooped the air above our garage.

Called Kate. Made a date.

Called Serenity. Made a re-date for a redo—tomorrow.

Called Jessica Trowley to check up on her.

Called Barbara. Not home yet from the hospital.

Jim called the police station. Still waiting for a call back.

Dinner was eaten, kitchen semi-cleared, and a couple of hours were spent in front of the television watching *Lewis*—a spin-off program from the popular *Inspector Morse* series set in Oxford—thus concluding the day.

In each detective program we had watched, the murderer was found within a few hours. Suspects were arrested and the rest of the people in town got on with their lives. That was not reality. Three and a half weeks had passed since Dan Swansey was murdered and dumped in the dumpster and the not-so-well-known Amy Miser had been left strangled in the barley field. Neither crime solved. Maybe we needed Lewis to visit East Lark. With his fortuitous luck we would have had both crimes solved in two hours, watched fourteen commercials, and used the loo at least twice. Wouldn't it be nice if, for once, what happened on television actually happened in real life?

Chapter Twenty

The numbers on the clock atop the cherry wood nightstand flipped. 03:01. So much for the sleeping tablets the doctor had given me.

Jim was fast asleep. His pipe-puffing lips were at work. Why could *he* sleep so soundly? Why could *he* not be miserable like I was? After all, misery loves company. I loved him. He was the only company I had; ergo he should be up with me.

For a quick second I was tempted to shake his shoulder and wake him. Maybe he would want to share a cuppa and a biscuit, and have a long chat about nothing whatsoever as I talked fast enough to break the sound barrier. Nope. Bad idea. He didn't like that when he had a good night's sleep. Why would I think he would enjoy the experience any more during the middle of the night when we were both groggy and ill-tempered?

03:25.

After tossing, turning, shuffling, and kicking—also known as midnight gymnastics—I'd had enough. I put on my bathrobe and went downstairs.

Not much activity was going on in the world at three-thirty in the morning. Stars still hung in the sky's canopy, but a slim layer of light glowed on the horizon. In spring and summer, when daylight savings time changed, morning behaved like a child who couldn't sleep and wanted to wake everyone else in the house so they could play. Looked like morning and I would keep each other company today.

I lifted the large Georgian window a tiny slit, letting some cool air sneak in, and wrapped my bathrobe tighter.

For several hours I drank coffee from my Queen mug and read *Break*. The warm java trickled through my veins as I relaxed in one of our soft living room chairs, waiting for Jim to wake.

Everything was so quiet it seemed I could hear the stars click off one by one.

+ + +

Next thing I knew Jim was shaking my shoulder, whispering my name. Morning must have played by itself after all.

The few hairs still clinging to life on his head resembled rabbit ears on an old-fashioned television.

"You're up early." He squatted by my chair.

Still waking, I asked, "What time is it?" I patted down his bunny hairs.

"Seven-thirty."

"I've been up for almost four hours."

"Are you okay?"

"Think so. The doc's tablets didn't help me sleep though."

"Anything bothering you?"

"Well, I did wake up thinking about Fred and Jessica."

He touched my hand. "That's why I don't like you getting involved in these things, Dotty. It's not good for you." He stood and went into the kitchen.

Daylight drenched the living room with prisms of white light. The day was in full bloom. I pushed the window down and followed Jim.

He poured boiling water into his cup with the teabag and let it steep for three minutes. Jim's exact approach to making one cup of Earl Grey tea was so precise it could earn him an Olympic medal.

I ignored his comment about not getting involved and poured more coffee into my drink now gone cold. "It dawned on me why Fred confessed to murdering Amy Miser. Do you remember when we were trying to help them through an argument one time?"

"Which one of the million times are you referring to?" He was still attending the tea, his back to me, the light-blue baggy pajamas he wore wearing thin. Next Debenhams sale I would have to get him a new set.

"The time when he told us he wished he could get Jessica's attention? How he wanted to make her realize he wasn't a lazy bum like she always said?" My coffee took effect. Everything seemed crystal clear. "He told us the only way he thought he could make Jessica realize how great a man he was, was by doing something she would never expect. I thought he was talking about getting a job or taking her away on a special holiday."

Jim carried his award-winning, gold-medal-making tea to the table. "Dotty, please slow down. You know my brain doesn't kick in as quick these days."

"Last night I kept thinking how Fred was incapable of murdering anyone, let alone a woman. If you think about it, he doesn't even have enough gumption to fry an egg."

"What's your point, Dotty?" He stirred, sipped, and swallowed: three more steps to a perfect cuppa.

"Well, that's when I remembered the conversation we had with them, how Fred wanted Jessica to look up to him. I didn't think anything of it at the time. Figured he was blowing smoke."

"I recall him saying something about wanting to impress her." Jim started his slow verbal engines with a kick in the pants from the Earl. Grey, that was.

"That's what I woke up thinking. How he could have seen the murders in the village as an opportunity to do that, to impress her. As sick as it sounds, maybe he said he murdered that woman to show Jessica he wasn't some deadbeat loser."

"Even Fred wouldn't be stupid enough to confess to murder to get her attention, would he?"

"He might have thought the police wouldn't believe him and would release him straight away. Still getting him some glory to brag about, but nothing more. I bet Fred didn't count on the police being desperate enough to want to solve these crimes that they accepted his confession at face value." I shook my head as the reality of the situation sank in. "How can we convince the police Fred lied about being a murderer to make himself look like a man in his wife's eyes?"

"As soon as we have breakfast I will clean up and call the police station again. I'll see about visiting Fred and find out where things stand with him, okay?"

I kissed him on the tip of his nose and patted his rabbit-eared hair one last time. "You're the best."

Chapter Twenty-One

After a quick change, I dashed to the hairdresser.

More than anything, I wanted a few hours with hair blowers screaming, women nattering, and scissors clipping—music to any woman's ears.

Fiona, the hairdresser, always made a silk purse out of a sow's ear. This time was no exception and I was pleased with my new "do."

Before heading home, I detoured to Peter's homegrown vegetable stand for some sixty-pence specials. Swede, carrots, and onions were on offer for half the price at Sainsburys. Homemade soup was on the checklist for tonight's dinner.

In spite of a 3:01 wakeup call I felt energized—not by Energizer Bunny standards, but it was a start.

Inside the house, a scribbled note sat on our kitchen table:

> *Dotty, I'm off to see Fred and talk with the police.*
> *Meet me at Hare and Hound at 7:00.*
> *See you then. Love, J*

Yeah. The vegetables could be saved for another day.

A new hairdo demanded a new ensemble, especially with an invite out to dinner. A bright red dress with white trim, quarter-length sleeves, and A-line style suited an ever-changing body like mine.

+ + +

Diminishing daylight filtered through the ancient leaded Hare and Hound windows.

Shop owner Jon, his wife, Carole, and their family were enjoying a meal, along with milkman Morris, postman Arty, and several others from the village. Arty chuckled and appeared more relaxed than the last time I'd seen him flinging mail into house slots. Everyone at the table had ordered fish and chips. I smacked my lips as heaping dishes of cod were placed in front of them.

Erika and husband, Jason—baby Addie sound asleep in his arms—waved from another table.

Lillie and Jake sat with a couple I'd never seen before. "Yoo-hoo, Dotty."

I waved and veered away.

Walter sat on a stool at the bar, unshaven, the comb-over not so combed over. His shirt was wrinkled, and he had slung his flowered tie over his shoulder. I had never thought of Walter as a heavy drinker, but it was obvious he'd been downing the pints.

The corner table where Jim and I sat during our last lunch was empty so I slid into a seat.

By seven-thirty the pub was full and Jim was half an hour late.

Each time the door swung open I'd glance over the menu to see if it was him. Each time it wasn't I chewed another fingernail. My palms were sweating, the black-inked menu smeared on my fingertips. Perfect for fingerprinting at a police station.

Maybe I should have gone with Jim to see Fred in prison instead of being selfish and going to the hair salon.

Surely no one would hurt Jim.

By eight o'clock I wiped tears away with a tissue.

The pub began to empty, as Arty, Jon, and Morris headed to the door. Arty touched the bill of his cap as he walked past and smiled.

Erika, Jason, and baby Addie had left a while ago.

Since the Hare and Hound was a family eatery, folks tended to come and go during early evening hours. The Queen's Treat, on the other hand, didn't start rocking 'til at least ten, when karaoke was the name of the game.

+ + +

Daylight was nearly gone and the pub's lighting changed to a deep hue of blues and purples. Votive candles in cheap glass holders were lit. Roger came and shrugged his shoulders, as if asking if I needed anything.

"No thank you."

Walter was still hunkered over the bar, another drink in hand.

The door creaked open one more time. I hesitated to look. I didn't want to be disappointed again. My nails were nearly gone.

Jim came through the door smiling.

I could have cried. Instead, I waved a serviette at him like a silly schoolgirl on her first date.

"Well, Mrs. Weathervane, you're looking pretty cute tonight. What's the occasion?" Jim sat, patted my hand, and read the smeared menu.

Relief turned to rage. "Jim Weathervane, where have you been?"

The few folks left in the pub turned our way. I lowered my voice. "I was so worried about you. What took you so long to get here? Why didn't you call? Didn't you know I'd be worried sick?"

"Traffic was bad. I couldn't call. The cell phone died. Yes. I knew you'd be worried." He touched my cheek. "I'm sorry to keep you waiting and worrying."

My helium-balloon-sized anger deflated, and I placed my hand over his. "I'm relieved you're okay."

"What would you like to eat?" Jim flipped the menu open. "I'm going to have the lasagna."

"I'd decided an hour ago on the mouth-watering fish swimming in vinegar." My stomach growled in agreement.

The aroma of fish and chips and Jim's lasagna floated toward us. Plates of fresh steamed veggies—carrots, broccoli, and cauliflower—came as side dishes with the main course.

We focused our attention on the task at hand—shoveling food—and dropped conversation for several minutes.

Jim swabbed the last of the pasta sauce off his plate with a piece of baguette.

"Did you manage to see Fred? What did the police say?"

"Yes, and it was exactly as you suspected. You'd make a fine detective, Dotty. Not that I'm encouraging you to pursue a career in it, mind you."

"What did Fred the fool say?"

"I couldn't believe what he told me." Jim shook his head. "Fred wanted to make Jessica jealous. He learned his lesson the hard way this time."

"I knew he was silly but that's beyond belief."

Roger came to our table, writing pad in hand, and we ordered our desserts without him having to say a word. We knew precisely what we wanted: a scoop of vanilla ice cream for Jim, Bramley apple pie slice floating in heavy cream for me, and two cups of tea to follow.

"What did the police say?" I tapped my fingertips together.

Jim flicked his eyes at me and at Roger, who continued to jot things on the pad. When Roger realized we'd stopped talking, he walked away. "That was strange. Why was he hanging around?"

"Oh, he probably wanted to write something down before he forgot. I do it all the time. Go on. What did the police say? Word for word. I want the nitty-gritty details."

"Once they cross-examined Fred, they knew he couldn't be their suspect."

"I could've told them that."

Roger returned and served our desserts with silent maneuvers, and hovered like a bee collecting pollen, picking up the salt and pepper shakers and malt vinegar. He lingered at the next table sorting placemats and putting extra linens away.

Jim waited until Roger left. "Turns out Fred had an alibi when both the murders were supposed to have been committed." He scooped a spoonful of ice cream into his mouth, closed his eyes, and moved his mouth with obvious pleasure before swallowing. "Several guys from the village confirmed he was with them at the banger-racing course both times. He even had a receipt in his wallet with time and date to prove it."

"That's a relief. So the police released him?" I bit into the warm pie.

"No. They kept him tonight for impeding a police investigation and to teach him a lesson."

"I bet Jessica will beat him with a rolling pin when she gets a hold of him. Or sticks him back in the garage to live on bread and water again for a few days. Or *maybe* she'll realize how much he loves her and start treating him with a bit of respect."

Jim scooped the last spoonful of ice cream into his mouth. "Fred isn't going to do anything stupid like that again for a long time."

"Let's hope so. Do they have any other suspects, then?"

He licked the spoon until it was clean enough for someone else to use. "Nope."

"So we're back to square one. Two murders—Dan Swansey and Amy Miser; two weapons—a bowie knife and necktie; Barbara Swansey on her kitchen floor; and no suspects, no solutions."

"Sure looks like it, Dot."

Lillie, Jake, and their friends stood at their table, scooped up jackets and always-handy-in-England umbrellas. Lillie waved goodbye to us with the movement of the Queen at her birthday parade. Jake trailed behind her and the other couple followed.

"With no further clues everyone around us is still suspect. Even Lillie could be our murderer." Jim winked and nodded toward the back of her as they walked out the door.

I giggled and tapped his arm. "At least with Fred cleared of the charges we won't be inundated with a million phone calls anymore. What a relief."

Roger brought our tea and removed the emptied dessert dishes.

Jim lifted his teacup. "Now, Mrs. Weathervane, how about we change the subject and talk about something else?"

I picked up my drink and held it out. "Cheers, Jim. I'm so grateful you're safe. This is indeed a special date with my mate. Maybe things will settle down now and get back to normal."

Jim tapped his cup with mine. "One can only hope."

Chapter Twenty-Two

Our little secret was out.

The police released the information, and the newspapers were quick to print that Jim and I had found both murder weapons.

Folks acted toward us like vultures circling freshly dead carcasses. Neighbors and strangers alike followed us wherever we went and picked at us for information.

The phone rang endlessly.

A lunch date with Kate at Molly's Tea Leaf was in order. It was her birthday, and I wanted to treat her to a special lunch. Plus, I wanted Kate to know firsthand why I hadn't told her earlier about finding the weapons.

We settled into our chairs in the upstairs area hoping for a quiet, uninterrupted time of nattering.

A woman with large dangling earrings and long, gray hair appeared at our table. "Aren't you Mrs. Weathervane? The woman who found the murder weapons?"

"Do I know you?"

"Um. No."

"Then I'm sorry. I'm busy with my friend here."

She strode away with a twist and a humph.

I wished I had thought to wear a baseball cap and dark glasses as several others stopped at our table. Instead we asked for a takeaway container and walked out with leftovers and indigestion.

+ + +

As the "vultures" hovered, Jim and I tried to maintain as much routine as possible.

I went to the shop for necessities—only to be accosted by reporters who wanted to know about the infamous murder weapons—and left empty-handed.

Jim headed out to his garden refuge. Tulip tips would soon open and magnolia tree blossoms resembled pink and white lips. The last thing that needed repairing was the hedge where the knife had been found; otherwise, the garden was coming along quite nicely.

Right now, though, Jim's haven was no heaven with the neighbors constantly pestering him. People passed by and shouted over the stone wall asking if he had found any other weapons. What did they think? He grew them?

Lillie called five or six times. Her concern seemed to grow into obsessive, compulsive behavior. I couldn't bear going over the same conversation repeatedly and stopped answering the phone.

"Let's take a ride to the coast, Jim." Going to the beach seemed a preferred option to the nonstop questions and endless phone calls. The only problem was that it was a bank holiday weekend. There were eight of these weekends a year in England, all officially adopted in 1871. Banks were closed and no trading occurred, thus the term "bank" holiday. Every hectare of beach would be covered with holidaymakers slathered in oil, worshipping an absent sun god, even though it was still only spring.

"No, thank you," Jim said. That took care of that.

We finally decided to stay inside, take the phone off the hook, and lie low like Br'er Rabbit for a few days until things calmed down.

But another problem turned up. The heat.

Spring burst into a hot summer wannabe.

Temperatures soared and our bodies baked, sizzled, and fried: great ways to serve chicken but not a great way to enjoy seclusion in a house with no air conditioning or cooling system. Air conditioners were normally not necessary in Britain, except for about three days a year. And we inadvertently chose those three days to shut ourselves in.

The one tank top and pair of shorts I owned came in handy. Chewing on a chunk of ice cube helped but only for a second. "Think I'm boiling to death."

"That's the fourth time you've said that in the last five minutes."

"How hot is it?" I dragged a piece of an ice cube across my forehead.

"For the fourth time, it's thirty degrees Celsius."

"What is that in Fahrenheit?" Never could do the math.

"Eight-six."

I folded a piece of paper into a makeshift fan. "That's unheard of in England this time of year."

Jim stood by the freezer with the door flung open and his head thrust inside, breathing in the cold air.

+ + +

We sneaked out to the garden when the sun had set, sipped iced drinks in the summerhouse, and watched cubic zirconia stars glitter against what looked like a backdrop of theatrical drape. Light glowed from a yellow citronella candle on the rattan table between us. In the semi-darkness we whispered to each other about the murders, weapons, Barbara Swansey, and others in the village. Who was the killer? Why East Lark? All the time we talked we worried neighbors lurked, listened, or would jump out any minute wondering what we were up to. We were trapped in or out. And neither option was pleasant.

Chapter Twenty-Three

After three days, we had had enough.

We gave up our daytime hideout and evening garden trysts.

The following day we turned on the phone, Jim went into the garden in broad daylight, and I walked to the shop for bread and juice.

We were finished being self-appointed prisoners.

Naturally the weather returned to dull, grey, and cool since we were no longer cloistered inside. Go figure.

Jim's torn jeans, rumpled green shirt, cap, and tattered gloves were once again the uniform of the day.

Secretly I vowed some day he would go looking for those clothes and find them missing. He and Sherlock would need to search for many clues before they found where I had dumped them. One place I would not choose would be the Queen's Treat dumpster; they'd discovered enough decomposed things there already.

It seemed while we were in seclusion, others got on with their lives and left us alone.

Snooping neighbors stopped snooping.

Even the local newspaper was back to reporting minor disturbances and primary school events.

Bliiiing.

Dare I answer the thing?

"East Lark, 58 1808," I said with apprehension, certain it was our neurotic neighbor, Lillie.

"Dotty, this is Barbara."

My womanly "antenna" went haywire. Was Barbara victim, vamp, or what? "Barbara, how nice of you to call. How are you?" I'd wondered periodically how she was doing since the night we found her lying on her kitchen floor. Was it an accident? Or had someone tried to harm her?

"I wanted to say thank you to you and Jim for saving me."

"You're welcome. We're glad we came when we did."

"Would you like to come over for some dessert and a cup of tea later? Why don't you come, say around seven, and bring Jim along? I wanted to thank him, too."

"That's sounds lovely. See you then."

+ + +

Barbara, dressed in speckled green and yellow baggy trousers resembling pajamas and a solid green top that matched her eyes, opened the door. Her Crest-like smile gleamed.

She seemed to have lost weight while recovering in the hospital. Maybe I should sign up for a stint in the medical center.

"Thank you so much for coming."

Several Yankee Candles glowed on the coffee table while classical music played in the background, a romantic setting for two rather than an informal gathering of three.

Barbara turned the music down and turned up the lights, but kept the candles lit.

We settled into her cozy living room, while she served us warm tea and slices of store-bought key lime pie from the base commissary—the packaging had been left on the kitchen counter.

National Trust brochures were still atop the mahogany coffee table by the candles. Her military bags were now put away.

Our conversation began awkwardly at first, as we spoke simultaneously.

"I want to thank you again for rescuing me," Barbara said.

"How are you feeling?" I asked.

"Did anyone want to hurt you?" Jim's question stopped Barbara and me in our verbal tracks.

"Why do you ask?" She peered over her delicate rose-flowered teacup. Steam from her drink left a mist in front of her face, blurring her expression. Was it puzzlement, fear, or maybe suspicion?

"We were worried about you, that's all."

Awkward silence pervaded the room.

"I feel so silly." She lowered her chin.

I leaned forward and touched her knee. "Please don't feel silly. What happened?"

"You aren't going to believe this."

"Try us."

She shrugged. "I consider myself pretty independent."

Was she desperate enough to commit suicide with Dan being murdered and perhaps being a suspect herself? Gently, I asked, "You didn't try to hurt yourself, did you?"

"What?" Up her head went. "Of course not."

Jim interjected. "If no one tried to hurt you and you didn't do it intentionally, what happened?"

"My mind has been in a muddle lately."

"That's understandable," I sympathized.

"When I arrived home from work that night I worked on a bunch of paperwork while fixing dinner at the same time."

That's why the kitchen was in such a state.

"The phone rang. I had a saucepan on the stove, went to turn it off, and saw there wasn't any flame under the pan. So I figured I mustn't have turned it on. After talking for about twenty minutes, I hung up and went to finish more work."

Barbara grabbed the band holding her ponytail in place and pulled it out, momentarily freeing her blond tresses, and retied it. "Guess I totally forgot I turned the burner on. The pilot light must have blown out and fumes filled the kitchen. I don't understand why I didn't smell anything. Guess I was so involved in what I was doing I didn't pay any attention. I feel so silly."

Jim relaxed in the chair and crossed his ankles. "Don't feel bad, Barbara. It's okay. It could happen to any of us."

Her eyes lifted and met mine. She turned to Jim. "Thank you both for being so kind. When I first met you in the shop, Dotty, you were so nice. But ever since Dan's . . ." Her voice shook.

"Barbara, things have been pretty tough for you, haven't they?" Jim's pastor voice soothed.

"It isn't just Dan's death. Things have been hard. A new assignment, Dan being gone, and well, let's say others in the village treating me as if I have leprosy."

"We're truly sorry for what's happened." I held her hand.

"Thank you," she whispered.

I released my grip. "Let me assure you it's hard enough to get to know people here when nothing bad has happened." I leaned back. "So it's no wonder you feel like folks shun you. It takes a while for the locals to warm up to new people on a good day, never mind when a tragedy's occurred."

"I wish I could get to know some of the villagers better. I've started off on the wrong foot here, I'm afraid."

"When everything dies down we'll get together and invite you over so you can meet some of them, okay?"

"That would be wonderful."

Barbara curled her legs under her like a wise sage sitting atop a mountain. I was envious of the move. I couldn't do it even if Jim helped me. And if he were successful, he would never get me unfolded again, and I would live forever a pretzel.

She abruptly changed the subject. "Why don't you tell me more about the people in East Lark?"

Although Barbara smiled, her jaw was tightly clenched and her fingers rolled in and out of a ball next to her thighs, as though she were trying hard to act casual.

Why did I have a sneaking suspicion she was digging for information, not discussing pleasantries about the locals? Here we were talking about her near-death experience at the hand of a pilot light, and she switches the subject as if we were talking about the weather—which was a popular topic in England. Don't know what to say to an Englishman? Mention the forecast.

Jim said, "Anyone in particular you want to know about?"

"How about Jon, the village shop owner?" She relaxed her posture, unfolded her legs, and sat back. "How long's he been here? He's always so helpful when I'm looking for something in the store."

Jon's totally shaved head, lean frame, and compact stature made him a good candidate for competitive swimming. I said, "Jon's been in the village about five years. Don't know much about where he's originally from, but you're right. He's nice."

"Is he married? Does he have a family?"

"Yes, his wife, Carole, is from the next village, and they've been married about ten years, I think. Jon's a true family man." I bit my tongue. Did I say something out of line about Jon being a "true family man" since Dan Swansey had been anything but?

Barbara didn't seem bothered by my unintentional slip.

"He and Carole have two small children. You can go past their house and see him playing with the kids outside or fixing their thatched cottage when they aren't working at the shop."

"How interesting." Barbara fingered a loose curl. "What about Walter Reed? I understand he's a retired magistrate?"

Now that's an odd question.

Walter seemed about as exciting as a cold piece of cod and a plate of mushy peas. Many of the locals had wondered about

Walter for years. But why in the world did Barbara want to know about him?

"All we know is he came to East Lark as a widower and worked part time in the judicial system when he moved here. Initially he'd flaunt his credentials, trying to impress everyone. No one paid much attention. Farmers don't have time to wonder what others have done previously."

A look of amusement crossed Barbara's face.

I lifted the tea cozy and poured more tea. "He settled into a small semi-detached on Eldo Road, pretty much staying to himself most of the time. He's shown up at village fetes, flower shows, or in the pub, but otherwise we rarely see him."

Jim added, "He's pleasant enough, but I get the feeling he's a pretty lonely guy."

"Pauline would be a good diversion for him. I would *love* to get the two of them . . ." Jim gave me "the look." Guess matchmaking Pauline and Walter would have to wait another day.

Barbara prodded, "How about Roger, the Hare and Hound owner?"

Jim said, "Not much to tell about him. Pretty quiet guy. Hardly ever hear him talk. Not married but runs a family-friendly place. That's about it."

Barbara asked about Arty, Morris, and Fred and Jessica. She wanted to know everything about them. Where did Fred and Jessica come from? Were they locals or outsiders? Did Fred work somewhere? What did Jessica do?

She probed with the intensity of a scope looking for a polyp.

Before we knew it, the questioning was over and she had us at the door saying a hasty goodbye.

We headed up the lane. The lights in Willow's End clicked off one by one, leaving the lane in darkness. I grabbed Jim's elbow. "What do you suppose that was about?"

"Not sure."

"She was digging for something, I'm sure of it. Jonesy wanted me to snoop around on Barbara, and it went the other way around, don't you think?"

"Um. Hm. Not sure."

"It's as if she were interrogating *us*, like she was a policewoman or agent of some kind. I was a bit intimidated when she slipped into her military mode of cross-examination. Weren't you?"

"Not sure."

I stopped. "Is that it?"

He slipped my hand from his elbow and held it. "I'm not sure I want to talk about it anymore either. Let's enjoy the walk home and see if we can point out some of the constellations on the way. Look, isn't that the Plow?"

"Plow? I thought it was called the Big Dipper."

"It's another name for it."

Jim opened our front door and we stepped into the darkened hall.

I normally enjoyed stargazing, but our conversation with Barbara had been disturbing, as if she were doing some big dipping, or was that big digging, herself?

Chapter Twenty-Four

We watched a rerun episode of *Inspector Morse*, shut off the lights, and went to bed.

Jim's lips puffed.

My forest green blanket and I tossed and turned together like a fresh spinach salad.

Numbers flicked on the clock. 11:28. 11:29.

The digits were mesmerizing and caused me to become drowsy. Either that or the tablets the doctor gave me finally kicked in. Whichever it was, I closed my eyes and slipped into a dream. Jim was dressed in an expensive tuxedo, cummerbund wrapped around his waist. I wore a long golden gown, low cut in the front. We were young again, dancing a waltz to guarantee us a spot on *Dancing with the Stars*, laughing at some joke.

BAM.

"What was that?" I bolted upright, the dream gone with a pop. "Sounded like a lorry rammed into our front window."

We stayed in bed for several minutes, not daring to breathe. We got up, donned our robes, and tiptoed down the stairs.

I clung to the back of Jim's robe. "What do you suppose that was?"

"Shhh." Jim pointed toward the living room, a large wrench securely in his hand.

We reached the hall landing. I squealed at my shadow in the hall mirror and grabbed Jim's robe.

"*Shhh.*"

I pulled him back toward me and whispered into the back of his head. "Why do you keep telling me to shush?"

"Someone might still be in here." He held the wrench higher.

"Oh no." I clung to his back with the grip of a leech on a large varicose vein.

We tiptoed inside the living room.

Two large Georgian windows, one on each end of the room, let both daylight and moonlight in, depending on the time of day.

Right now there was neither. It was too early for daylight, and any moonlight was hidden behind a cloud.

We flipped on the light switch.

"Oh, no," I muffled into my hands.

Jim lowered the wrench. "Who'd do that?"

"I can't believe someone could be so mean."

"*Why* would someone do it?"

The front, beautiful replica-Georgian glass was totally collapsed onto the settee as if it had imploded.

Cool air whistled through the room. Papers flew like overgrown butterflies hovering around a buddleia: a beautiful flowering plant, named after Reverend Adam Buddle, a botanist and rector in Essex. Jim had given me a lesson on buddleias just the other day—otherwise I wouldn't have known or cared.

Jim rang the police. Again.

They were going to get tired of hearing from us. What in the world would they say when we called this time?

We closed the door to the living room, put the kettle on, and waited for PC Jones to arrive.

+ + +

The pot percolated, the kettle boiled, and Jim and I steamed over what someone had done to our lovely home.

I blew into a hanky. "Who could've done this?"

"Don't worry, Dot. Everything will be okay."

"I'm so mad and upset, I don't know which to be first."

"We can be grateful no one was hurt." Jim—the optimist.

He poured me a cup of coffee in my Queen mug and began his Earl Grey ritual.

"But why would anyone want to do this? We don't have any enemies here that I know of. And this has always been such a quiet place. What would compel someone to break the window? What did we do to deserve this?"

Jim put a hand on my shoulder and gently squeezed, his simple touch as soothing as aloe on a bad burn. "Dotty, I don't know who did this, but believe me, I will find out. And I'll make sure they're prosecuted to the full letter of the law." Jim's military bearing kicked in. He had been provoked to a stage of anger, a rare phenomenon for him.

The kitchen clock read 12:30 when the doorbell rang.

Constable Jones stood at the door looking frazzled, confusion combined with tiredness making her small face appear distorted.

Funny what you think about when you're under stress. For some strange reason Jonesy appeared much shorter than usual and would make a great stand-in for a munchkin in *The Wizard of Oz*. I glanced at her feet to be sure she wasn't wearing bedroom slippers.

She yawned. "What's happened with you two now?"

"PC Jones, good to see you." I pulled up the collar of my robe.

She tilted her head. "Where have you been the last few days?" Then stifled another yawn. "I haven't seen you around. Were you away?" She cupped her mouth as she finished another mouth-gaping stretch. "Must say I've been a bit worried."

As we escorted her into the living room, I answered, "We decided to stay indoors for a few days. We were tired of being hounded by everyone asking stupid questions."

Her eyes widened like two full moons when she saw the mess, as if she suddenly woke up. "Goodness. What's happened here?"

Jim said, "We heard a loud bang, came downstairs, found this mess, and called you."

"What a shame, and so strange. That someone would do this to you two. You're so liked in the village." She paused, as if speaking to herself, then said, "Wonder if this has anything to do with the murder weapons. Could someone be trying to scare you?"

I clutched Jim's arm.

Jonesy thin black eyebrows met in the middle of her brow. "We need to solve these crimes before anyone else gets hurt or any more damage is done. Something else happened earlier tonight that was odd, too. There was a break-in at the village hall. Locks were broken where the workers were fixing the back of the building. We've had to put a temporary lock on the thing until a proper locksmith gets there." She knelt over the shattered glass to get a closer look.

I said to Jim, "How in the world did we get so caught up in something you never wanted us to get involved with in the first place?"

He stood toe to toe with me, fists on his hips. "Could it be because you wanted to *help*, Dot? You're always saying you can't help it. But think about it. So far you've helped Barbara by saving her life, and you've helped Jessica by saving Fred from being hanged over murders he never committed. I'm not angry with you, Dotty . . ."

"I know, I know. You worry about me." I reached up and touched his rabbit-eared hair.

Jonesy straightened and opened her pad. "Have you spoken to anyone recently, in spite of your seclusion at home? Maybe someone on the phone?"

"Jim and I went to see Barbara last night. She invited us over to say thanks for helping her out."

"How's she? Did you find out anything?"

"No. But she sure was interested in certain folks in the village."

"Hm. Wonder why." Jonesy became lost in thought and mumbled under her breath. She mentally returned and changed the subject. "We'll send someone over in a few hours to take fingerprints. See what we can discover in daylight. In the meantime, try and get some sleep and keep the door to your lounge locked."

"Thank you, Constable Jones." Jim's voice softened as he accompanied her to the front door.

There was nothing else we could do until morning, so we both trudged back to bed hoping to regain some lost REM.

I wanted to get back to the romantic *Dancing with the Stars*.

Instead, we both lay flat on our backs, eyes wide open until dawn.

Chapter Twenty-Five

I bolted upright. The digits read 07:58.

Jim's side of the bed was cold to the touch.

A strong smell of brewed coffee wafted around the room, and I wiggled my nose like Peter Rabbit in Mr. McGregor's garden.

My chipped cup sat on the bedside table, and wispy white vapor spiraled upward. God bless Jim and God bless the Queen.

Bliiiing.

I grabbed the cradled phone sitting by the cup.

"Dotty, this is Lillie." Her voice pierced through the drug-induced stupor. The doc's sleeping tablets had done the trick. "Are you okay? Do you want me to come over and help clean up the mess?"

How was it possible she already knew about the window? That was fast even for her.

"Lillie, how in the world did you find out so quickly?"

She didn't bother answering. "I'm making dinner for you tonight, so you don't have to worry about fixing anything. I'm so upset for you both." Her words choked and she sniffled into an unseen tissue. She cleared her voice. "Who in the world would do something like this to you two? I'm so sorry this has happened."

"Thanks, Lillie. I appreciate it, but—"

The sniffles stopped and she rediscovered her authoritarian voice. "I'm not taking 'no' for an answer. I will stop by around six with roast beef and Yorkshire pudding."

"That's so kind," I spoke to the dull tone humming on the phone. Lillie had hung up.

Bliiiing.

I picked up the phone again, but before I had a chance to say anything, Kate piped in. "Dotty! What in the world happened? Are you and Jim okay? Can I bring you anything? What do you want me to do to help?"

When Kate and I first met at Serenity Salon she was formal and constrained. The longer I'd known her, the more she had picked up my quirks—like asking multiple questions in one breath. Poor Kate. Wish it had been the other way around and I had copied her posh traits instead.

"Kate, we're fine. The police are coming to take fingerprints and Lillie's bringing dinner later. But how in the world did you find out? It only happened a few hours ago."

"Everyone's talking about it."

"How did they know?"

"I'm not sure. But it certainly was the buzz when I was in the queue at the shop. I was buying some cereal and milk when I overheard Carl and Jon nattering about it like two old nannies. Do you know who did it?"

Someone was keeping a close lookout on us and spreading news quicker than jelly on toast. I stretched out and flicked on a lamp.

The odor of coffee drew my attention from the conversation for a brief second. All I yearned for was just one gulp.

"We don't have any idea, Kate. Jonesy was here earlier. But other policemen are coming to take fingerprints around the living room. So we have to get dressed and ready for them. I'd love for you to come over. Maybe you could help me clear up some of the mess."

"I'll stop by in about an hour."

I lingered long over the coffee, snuggled back under the bedcovers, and allowed myself a few more dreamy minutes.

+ + +

The fingerprint crew turned up.

I dressed quickly and turned up—with an idea.

Jim thought our current sofa was fine, but I wanted a new one. The old rose and cream settee was faded and worn and covered in broken glass. A great reason to move out the old and bring in the new. There was always something to be grateful for even in difficult times, if you looked hard enough.

When the police moved the furniture to figure out how the window was broken, they found several dust bunnies large enough for God to create a whole new breed of mankind, but nothing else.

Kate arrived to help, and after a quick cup of coffee for me and tea for her we began the business of clearing up.

Jim moved furniture back into place, picked up rubbish—the papers in a neat pile—and headed out to the garden.

Bliiiing.

Please don't let it be Lillie.

"Dotty, this is Barbara. I heard about the incident in your home. I'm so sorry and wondered if I could stop by and help?"

"How sweet of you. Kate left a minute ago and Lillie's bringing dinner over. So things are getting back to normal, but you're welcome to stop by."

"Wonderful. I'll see you later on."

As I hung up, the doorbell rang.

Walter Reed—dressed in gray pinstriped trousers held up with a set of yellow suspenders, and a starched white shirt too tightly fitted around his chubby neck—thrust a drooping bouquet of sunflowers at me.

His ensemble was complete with a yellow dotted tie, eyeglasses perched on the ball of his nose, and a notebook tucked under his arm.

"Why, Walter, what an unexpected surprise. Please come in."

"Dotty, I thought you and Jim might appreciate some legal advice. Heard you had some vandalism last night." If he'd had his gavel, I imagined he would have pounded it on the kitchen counter with hearty enthusiasm.

"How kind. I'm sure we would appreciate any help you could offer."

Wonder if he's offering his services for other reasons. He's never come by here before.

Was he trying to find out what we knew about the goings on in the village? Including the murders? Maybe he wanted to engage others and offer his judicial services for a price and we were his means of getting there. He'd been sitting pretty close to us at the pub the other day and could have easily overheard our conversation. He was pretty soused though, so I couldn't imagine he retained much.

I directed him outside to where Jim worked. "Thank you so much for the flowers."

He blushed crimson, the ball on his nose resembling a large cherry, and went outside.

Within minutes, he and Jim sauntered in, Walter sporting a large smile. Jim grabbed his light beige coat and flung it over his shoulder. "We're going to the Hare and Hound for a pint. Walter has some interesting stuff he's telling me."

When they opened the front door, Lillie flew into the house without stopping and rushed into the kitchen with a steaming pot. "Made stew instead of roast beef and Yorkshire. Can't stay, though. Have to get back to Jake and the farm."

"Lillie, thank you so much."

She whizzed past to leave, screeched to a halt, and spun back. "I'm truly sorry this happened to you." Her eyes flashed bright as if a light bulb snapped on in her head. "I'm wondering if maybe we *should* have another Neighborhood Watch meeting? Something strange is going on in our sweet village. And I for one am not going to stand for it." Without waiting for a response, she flew out the door.

Now how is she going to have another meeting with the village hall closed?

There was no time to worry about that right now.

The aroma of beef stew filled the house. Food was made to counter misery. Come to think of it, food was made for good days, bad days, any day of the week.

Ding dong.

I opened the door. "Barbara, come in."

The house was like a revolving door at Harrods during the Christmas rush.

"Was that Lillie Bakersfield flying down the road?" Barbara grinned knowingly. If she didn't know anything about anyone else in the village, she obviously had heard plenty about Lillie.

Barbara was dressed in gym gear and sneakers. An oversized gray hoodie with a silver New York emblem was opened over a black Under Armour T-shirt.

Bliiiing.

I pointed to the kettle. "Would you mind starting the water while I get the phone?"

"Sure." She slid off the hoodie and draped it across a chair at the table.

"East Lark, 58 1808, this is Dotty."

Two short bursts of air and the caller hung up.

"That was weird." I stared at the phone.

Every time Barbara and I began anew, the phone rang again.

Each time the same thing happened. Bursts of air, and the caller hanging up. I shut the ringer off.

"Guess I'll have to report this to Jonesy, too." I poured the hot water into a cup with an herbal teabag and passed it to her.

"Dotty, I'm sorry you've been caught up in everything. Do you think the breaking of your window was a coincidence?" She added two cubes of sugar and stirred. "Maybe those phone calls are from the same person who threw something through your window. Could it be someone's out to hurt you and Jim, or at least scare you?" Her shoulders shuddered.

Because of the broken window, a cross breeze had slipped along the hall and into the kitchen, cooling the house off. Jim had found a tarp in the shed and had used it as a temporary cover for the front window, but it was a haphazard repair.

Barbara slid her hoodie back on and crossed her arms. "All these things could be related to the murders. Maybe you and Jim should go away for a few weeks until everything settles down. Of course it might be hard with the smashed front window."

My throat constricted as if a fishbone was stuck in it. "Why do you think anyone would be interested in bothering with us?"

A few weeks ago the biggest complaint I had was the evil magician leaving piles in our kitchen. Now there were bigger things for concern. Instead of worrying who wanted to hurt the Swanseys, I worried who wanted to hurt us.

Barbara stared past my shoulder, her hands clasped around the cup. She shook her head as if trying to get rid of a thought. "Well, you and Jim *did* find the two murder weapons. Maybe the killer thinks you're on to something?" She lowered her drink and leaned on her elbows. "Could these things be tied together somehow?"

Goose bumps tingled across the small hairs on my arms. "Jonesy said the same thing, and I'm beginning to wonder about the possibility myself."

Barbara grabbed my arm. "Dotty? Are you all right?" She squeezed too hard, and I pulled away.

The Westminster clock in the living room struck the quarter hour.

"What? Oh yes, I'm fine." I bit my lip.

"Try not to worry too much." Her Crest smile turned strangely lopsided. "I'm sure everything will be okay. As long as you don't let yourself get too personally involved." The words seemed to roll off her tongue with sugary hostility.

I suddenly saw Barbara with new eyes. There seemed to be something cunning about her. Why hadn't I noticed it before?

Was I mistaken in thinking she was innocent, too nice to be involved with her husband's murder simply because she had pretty eyes and a Barbie doll physique? She could be the murderer and had even have faked her own fainting spell. Was everything a cover-up to divert attention from herself onto us?

I tried to push aside any doubts, but there was something not quite right about this gorgeous blond dressed in a New York hoodie. Any appetite I had was suddenly gone. Lillie's stew would have to wait for another day.

Chapter Twenty-Six

I pulled the kitchen curtain aside, and rain clattered sideways against the French windows.

Two blackbirds with bright orange beaks hopped around the grass, fishing for breakfast: warm, juicy worms. *Glad I wasn't born a bird.*

The garden was getting back to normal. Hopefully there wouldn't be a necessity for me to play water boy for Jim, filling watering cans in the sink, now that the plants were reestablished and the rain persisted.

I bent and stretched. Another morning exercise completed.

After a good night's tablet-induced sleep, a new day brought bright optimism in spite of the grim grayness.

As loud as I could, I sang Simon's "I Am a Rock." Paul Simon's songs were never more out of tune than when I had a go at them.

I might've overreacted about Barbara last night. She acted strange, though.

Seemed I considered everyone with suspicion: first, Walter with his saggy sunflowers, and second, Barbara with her odd smile. My emotions were on pins and needles. With the window smashing and the police spending half the day in the house, anyone's confidence would be on edge.

Jim whistled and bounced down the stairs to begin his Olympic Earl Grey routine. He stopped in his tracks when he heard me singing.

I turned on the radio and stopped my noise.

Poached eggs on granary bread and the Queen Elizabeth mug sat together on the table awaiting royal attention.

I will not let anything get to me today.

"Jim?"

The paper nodded and shook. An advert for Sainsbury's shuffled with the move. If the milk in the jug on the picture were real, there would have been white liquid everywhere.

"Now don't get upset."

Down the paper went. "Dotty, how many times do I have to tell you not to start a conversation with that statement? I expect to get upset if you tell me not to. Try again, please." Up the paper went.

"Jim?"

As if lowering a flag from a pole, Jim slowly dropped the paper to his lap. His eyes rolled and held impatience, but he kept his tone even. "Yes, Dotty?"

"I said 'don't get upset' because it's the only time you drop the paper and pay attention." First morning marital chess move made.

"Touché, Dot." Up the paper went.

"Jim, I really do want your attention."

Paper down. "Am I going to get upset?"

"Maybe." I tried a winsome smile. "Only, I've been thinking about something since the window was broken." I sped up. "The sofa's covered with glass and maybe we should replace it. Get a leather sofa to match the side chairs."

"Fine." Up the paper went.

I pulled the paper down in the center. "Gotcha," he said, and winked. His imaginary chess piece knighted mine.

I poured another cup of coffee, grabbed my blue trimmed with fake diamond chips reading glasses, and scanned the newspaper inserts. Every woman's favorite word was in bold primary colors—SALE—a furniture discount was going on at Harvey's. Life was indeed looking up. So far I had performed my morning exercise, Jim agreed to buy a sofa without an argument, plus a furniture sale. What more could a woman possibly want?

Ding dong.

"Should I try and pick up some of the mess?" I said.

"You don't have all day to answer the door." Jim chortled behind the printed page. I flicked the newspaper with my fingertip, and the paper hit the tip of his nose.

"Why, good morning, Chief Inspector O'Reilly and Constable Jones. Come in before you get soaking wet."

They shook their caps and stepped inside, and I hung their raincoats on hallway hooks.

"We didn't call you, did we?" I teased.

Neither spoke as I escorted them to the kitchen.

"Perfect timing on your part. Jim is fixing the best Earl Grey in East Lark. I'm sure you'd love one?"

"We don't have time," O'Reilly answered. This was indeed serious business to turn down a cup of tea on a wet, damp day.

My enthusiasm was squelched. "Not another murder, is there?"

"No. But what makes you ask?" the chief inspector snarled.

How can someone so handsome have such a devilish look? I hope Jonesy hasn't gotten too attached to this fellow. He's not worth it.

O'Reilly would certainly be a tough guy to live with, regardless of his good looks. His behavior was unpredictable. I was never sure whether he was for or against us.

We moved from the kitchen to the living room, now tidied from most of the broken glass and strewn papers. As wind blew through small slits in the window's tarp, the noise resembled a parent giving "raspberries" on a baby's belly.

Jim and I sat on the two leather chairs.

Chief Inspector O'Reilly sat on the edge of the sofa.

Jonesy stood behind him near the window.

Wish he'd sit on a piece of glass.

"Ouch," O'Reilly yelped and pulled a small shard from the back of his calf.

I put a hand over my mouth.

His frown deepened. "Mr. and Mrs. Weathervane, we need to know where you both were the night Dan Swansey was killed. Can anybody verify your whereabouts?" He flipped open his pad. His pencil pierced the air with those sword-thrusting movements.

"What? Why in the world would you ask us that?" Jim stood, fists forming.

"Please sit down."

I touched Jim's thigh and he sat, his fists opening and closing rapidly.

"It appears no one else in the village knows as much as you two about what is going on with these murders. After all, you found both murder weapons. How did you know where to look? And you found Barbara Swansey on her floor. At least that's what you said. But you only have each other as alibis."

He pointed to the black tarp whipping behind his head. "I'm not convinced you aren't responsible for this window shattering either." His Irish brogue sounded more like bagpipes gone rusty. "All of this could be an ingenious way of diverting attention from your own involvement with these crimes."

The octave of his voice deepened. He bent slightly at the waist, his attitude colder than built up frost in a freezer. "After all, what does anyone know about the two of you?" He sat back, straightened his spine. "So can you tell me where were you the night Dan Swansey was killed and do you have anyone who can verify it?"

I looked at Jonesy. "You can't be serious?" She looked down at the floor.

My eyes tried to pry hers up. I spoke to O'Reilly through clenched teeth. "If you knew Jim, you wouldn't even consider he had anything to do with a murder." I patted Jim's knee. "You'd know he couldn't hurt a spider or a fly."

I wanted to add: As for me, I don't have any trouble getting rid of a spider and periodically I might fly off the handle. In fact, I could seriously hurt your pretty face right about now, Chief Inspector.

"We were both home, and no, no one can verify it." Jim's jaw tightened, and he worked hard at maintaining his composure.

I piped in, "Why in the world would we kill Dan Swansey? We didn't even know the man. How could you think we had anything to do with this? Who do you think we are anyway?" O'Reilly didn't realize he had come up against the fastest question slinger in the west.

Jim touched my hand.

Jonesy stretched on her tippy-toes, trying to peek over the chief inspector's shoulder to read his notebook. He frowned up at her. She plopped back into place.

"Mrs. Weathervane, we have to consider each and every possibility. We'll need both of you to come down to the police station for further questioning."

They waited for us to gather our things: handbag, raincoats, umbrellas, and keys to the car. At least we were allowed to follow our accusers to the station in our own vehicle.

A song of cheerful optimism with Simon's "I Am a Rock" in the morning in spite of the clattering rain ended on a sour note. Where had we gone wrong minding our own business? Instead of enjoying a quiet retirement, we found ourselves completely embroiled in this whole mess, accused of two murders, and headed to the police station for questioning.

Chapter Twenty-Seven

We sat at a cold metal table on two uncomfortable chairs.

The plain gray room with one mirrored wall seemed to move in on us each time the single door opened and closed. My shoulders turned inward to stem the tide of claustrophobia.

Jim's forehead beaded with sweat. Periodically he swept a brow with fingertips and wiped his hand on his trousers.

The police interrogation resembled a one-act scene from *Groundhog Day*.

First one policeman came in the room, asked questions, and left. Another entered, then another, each going through the same litany:

"Mr. and Mrs. Weathervane, why did you choose East Lark to retire?"

"Do you know Dan and Barbara Swansey? Amy Miser?"

"Where were you on such and such a day, at such and such an hour?"

Jim responded every time with the same, even tone, "We came to East Lark because we wanted to find a place to enjoy a quiet retirement. My grandparents were English and when I was stationed here many years ago we enjoyed the countryside and locals."

Each officer nodded—resembling bobbing heads on car dashboards—and exited the room. Another policeman came in and repeated the process.

One by one they asked about Barbara.

I answered, "We know her a little, but we didn't know her before she and Dan were stationed here. When her husband died, we were trying to be kind. How dare you imply . . ."

When Jim sensed I was about to verbally assault someone, he grabbed my hand under the table and squeezed. Trying to keep a lid on my temper was comparable to someone trying to cork Mt. Vesuvius with a toothpick.

"Tell us again your occupation," yet again another police officer asked.

"I'm a retired service member," Jim tolerantly answered once more. "No, we did not know Dan Swansey or Amy Miser."

As time passed and questions continued, I sensed Jim's military bearing beginning to kick in. The knuckles on his clamped hands atop the table whitened, and his voice lowered. No one else might have noticed the slight changes in his demeanor, but I remembered them clearly from those years he marched in cold wet weather and gave orders. Even nonplussed Jim could only take so much before being fed up.

We were finally released and told not to leave East Lark, "in case we have any further questions."

Where did they expect us to go anyway?

I growled when Jim opened the passenger car door for me.

Jim focused on the road as he drove us home, hard-tapping fingers on the wheel a strong indicator of his frustrations at our humiliation at the hands of the police.

A pigeon the size of a small football flapped frantically in front of the car's fender, barely managing to fly by without having its wings clipped.

Rapeseed fields, grown to produce canola oil, were beginning to ripen. Soon stretches of sunshine-yellow rows would extend as far as the eye could see.

"Where did they get the idea we could have been involved in a murder?" I snarled, rolling down the window for some fresh air.

I inhaled deeply.

Sampson's pig farm was going through spring-cleaning of animal waste in preparation for birthing of piglets. Although the farm was several miles away, the stench was as strong as a year's supply of dirty socks fermenting in a hamper.

I gagged and rolled up the window. "Someone is out to frame us. Maybe it's the same person who told the reporters about you finding the knife, and whoever spread the news about the breaking of our window."

Jim clamped the steering wheel tighter. "But who do we know who'd want to frame us?"

"Well, it's either that or Chief Inspector Sean O'Reilly is out to make a name for himself. Did you notice how he moved around the police station like a cock around hens? We're his link to the murders. He's probably getting annoyed at the slow speed of the investigation, and questioning us made him look good." I swallowed hard to stem the taste of rising bile.

By the time we entered the house I'd formulated a plan.

"Dotty, watch your blood pressure," Jim reminded me as I hurled my handbag onto the kitchen counter. Papers flitted skyward.

"Yes, I know at 'my age' I have to watch *everything*. But the last thing I'm worried about is my blood pressure."

I slapped the counter, hitting the side of the perched handbag. It tipped over the edge and landed upside down on the floor.

I lifted the bag by the upturned bottom, and the contents escaped like prisoners from Alcatraz.

Grrrr. I was going to change bags anyways. Might as well do it now.

Before reaching the landing Jim called, "Dotty, what's this?" Reentering the kitchen, Jim held an envelope toward me.

"Don't know."

"I picked it up from your handbag debris."

"It's probably junk mail." I shrugged and turned to leave.

"Come here. Please. You'd better take a look." He gave me the envelope. "Dan Swansey's name is written on it."

"Oh, no." I sat, nearly missing the kitchen chair.

Jim grabbed my arm and guided me into the seat. "What is it?"

I dropped the envelope on the table as if handling burning coal. "I can't believe what I've done."

"Dotty, what's this letter?" He put a glass of water in front of me. "Where did it come from?"

I took a long gulp. "I found it at the same time I found the necktie with the nylons on the way to Serenity. I thought maybe Arty dropped it when he was in a hurry delivering mail." I picked the envelope back up and spoke to the sealed letter. "But I found the tie and forgot about this. It must have gotten buried in the bottom of the bag when I changed it and stuff shuffled around." I looked up at Jim. "What should I do?"

He fixed a long silver curl that had flipped out of place over my eye, and lifted my chin. "The first thing to do, Dotty Weathervane, is to get smaller handbags." He touched my cheek tenderly. "We're going to take the letter to the police. That's what we're going to do."

"If we take this to the police they'll wonder if we're involved in these murders. Chief Inspector O'Reilly doesn't need anything else to convince him we're somehow responsible. That man makes my blood boil." I shook the envelope in the air. "If we show up with this letter with Dan's name on front, we're sure to be tossed into prison for life." I threw the letter on the table with renewed anger mixed with fear.

Jim sat. "What do you think we should do then?"

I jumped from the chair and stomped toward the stairs. "After I get another handbag, I'm going to clean up this mess." I made it halfway up the stairs and shouted back, "Then I'm going to make some phone calls. We have to clear our names."

After years of marital chess, Jim knew better than to disagree during times I was worked up over something. This would definitely be one of those times.

Rummaging through my purse collection, I came across the Cath Kidston that Kate had given me for my last birthday and to celebrate my official status as an old age pensioner.

I tromped back to the kitchen and put miscellaneous things from the upturned purse into the Kidston. Several items: used receipts, tissues, three finished lipstick tubes, and a variety of other useless objects went into the bin. Another golf ball I'd picked up from the front garden and shoved into my purse went into a kitchen drawer. It was the third one I'd found.

Jim knew when to leave well enough alone and hid out in the summerhouse with his gardening books.

Finishing up the mess and rinsing out the QE mug for coffee, I began to dial.

There were moments in life when it was necessary to call on friends to come alongside during times of trouble. And we were in a heap of trouble.

"Hello, Kate. This is Dotty. I need your help."

Before the day was over I had called Lillie and Jake, Fred and Jessica, and Walter and asked them to come over the following morning. I wanted Walter's legal advice on what to do with the letter.

It was once stated: "God specializes in using little-known people and lightly valued objects to accomplish great feats for His purpose." Tomorrow, a group of little-known people would meet to accomplish a great feat the police had not been able to do—solve two murders and find the killer or killers in our midst.

Chapter Twenty-Eight

As soon as the shop opened in the morning I was there, black umbrella and wallet in hand, and I purchased a selection of biscuits for our small gathering.

In spite of the drizzle, the day was mild. A small patch of blue sky poking through the clouds over the airbase promised sunshine.

The golden retriever from Number Ten was now attached to a leash held by a lanky lad with a Beatle-type haircut. I thought long and shaggy went out with the sixties. His head hung and a hawk-shaped nose poked out. They say pets resemble owners and these two made a perfect match. I couldn't tell who was walking whom.

Barbara pulled her Z-3 to the curb in front of the shop. The red bonnet of the car was spotted with small droplets from the morning mist.

I ducked under the umbrella so she wouldn't see me as I passed. I still wasn't sure where I stood with her. Was she concerned or calculating?

Once home, I sorted the biscuits on a plate and started the kettle.

First to arrive were Lillie and Jake.

Lillie carried her tapestry bag. A large ball of variegated yarn pierced with knitting needles sat on top. She set the bag down, took off her Miss Marple hat, and hugged me several seconds. She pulled back, her hands still holding me. "Thank you so much for asking us to come. This whole affair has been so hard on everyone. But especially you two." She let go, picked up her bag and hat, and headed into the living room.

Jake stood in the doorway. He clasped Jim's hand and shook, both nodding in understanding. How was it that women took a thousand words, physical contact, and tears to express themselves to others? All it took a man was a handshake.

Lillie and Jake sat together on the sofa in front of the still broken window.

Window repairmen had come, taken measurements, and given a quote but it would take days for the glass to be cut and fit. In the meantime, we put up with the whistling tarp. Used to the noise, I periodically sang Paul Simon's "Bridge Over Troubled Water" with the tarp's sound as acoustical accompaniment, much to Jim's dismay.

Ding dong.

"Hello, Walter." He wasn't wearing his usual formal attire of starched shirt and tie. I had never seen him without either. Instead, a short-sleeved bright-checked shirt was buttoned all the way to his neck.

Come to think of it, it was a tie that killed Amy Miser—I shook my head to rid the thought. My imagination had definitely gotten out of hand.

Walter carried a notebook tucked under his arm. Seeing him hunched over a pint the other evening in the pub seemed out of character.

What happened for him to drink so much?

I led him into the living room. "Thank you for coming. I know you'll be a huge help."

He blushed and sat in one of the leather chairs. "Happy to be here."

Jim took coffee and tea orders.

Fred and Jessica sauntered up the path. I opened the door before they had a chance to ring the bell. "Please come in. Thank you so much for coming at such short notice."

Locked hand in arm, they entered the sitting room with a bit of hesitation.

They nodded to Jake and Lillie but stepped back when they saw Walter. Fred seemed a bit gun-shy of anyone or anything to do with police—including a retired magistrate—after his antics at confessing to the murder of Amy Miser.

I moved them further into the room with a slight push on Jessica's back.

Walter smiled and they seemed to relax.

Jim served Lillie and Jake tea and Walter coffee. He returned with a plate of the store-bought biscuits. Lillie grabbed a chocolate-covered Hob Nob. The small, light hairs over her top lip wiggled as she nibbled. Jake and Walter declined.

Fred and Jessica acted as out of place as if they had entered Buckingham Palace. They snuggled together on the sofa by Lillie and Jake.

Jessica's normally harsh bitter face had softened after Fred's confession of murder. She was actually attractive since she toned down her makeup. Her tattooed ankles showed below mid-calf shorts. My only complaint was the revealing bodice top with its spaghetti straps and low-cut laced trim dipping into her mountainous cleavage.

Fred stretched out and bounced his legs with nervous energy. Jessica patted his stick-thin leg with her chubby hand, a silver ring on each finger. He stopped the bounce and crossed his ankles.

The one person missing was Kate.

Ding dong.

Kate was back to herself—from the frazzled look when she came to announce the death of Amy Miser to the normally meticulous person I knew. Her hair was neatly parted and in place, and she wore a pale blue Laura Ashley skirt with a printed blouse.

We hugged.

"Dotty, this meeting is ingenious." She released me. Her dimpled cheek deepened. "As a group, we can get more accomplished than you and Jim trying to go it alone." She entered and sat on the remaining leather chair beside Walter's.

After everyone was served tea or coffee and plates of cookies, Jim said, "Can we please get started?"

The murmur in the room halted.

Even without the chance to drink a full pot of coffee I was ready to get the show on the road. The sooner we figured out some details for the police, the sooner they would leave Jim and me alone.

I hadn't entirely convinced Jim this meeting would work. Yet I couldn't help but think he had come to the realization we were knee-deep in the murder-briar-patch and needed to do something. Otherwise, he wouldn't have agreed to help out.

He glanced at his calloused hands and cleared his throat. "First of all, thank you all for being here. As you know, we were at the police station yesterday being questioned. We realized after our time with them that they're not having much luck solving these murders." Jim had a politer way than I did of saying we thought O'Reilly was an inept clod. "So, we wanted to solicit your help. Perhaps find out some answers to some unresolved questions.

"Dotty has come up with a list of things for each one of us to do, if you agree. Why don't you tell us what you have in mind, Dot?" Jim sat back in the folded chair he had brought in from the garage and placed his palms on his knobby knees.

"Thank you, Jim." I scanned the room at the motley crew assembled: tall "Ichabod" Fred and chunky Jessica; Lillie, the Miss Marple wannabe, and Jake, her yes-man; stiff-necked Walter; and graceful Kate. They might be an unlikely set of sleuths but they were the only ones I had, and somehow I knew I could count on them for whatever I needed.

"What I propose is giving each of you a task. If you don't feel you can help or don't want to take on the particular job I've assigned, please let me know. Maybe we can find something more suitable for you to do, if you're willing?"

Everyone nodded.

"Lillie." As soon as I mentioned her name she sat straighter in the chair as if a bolt of electricity had struck her from underneath. Cookie crumbs fell from her lap onto the floor. She grabbed a notebook and pen from her tapestry bag and was poised ready to write, humorless and intent as she waited for instructions.

"Would you hunt around for more information on Amy Miser? Where did she come from and how did she end up in this area? Seems no one knows anything about her. Is she British? Some other nationality? I'm afraid you're starting from scratch on this one."

She wrote furiously.

"I'm not sure how you'll go about finding out anything, but if anyone can discover something, I'm sure you can." I did not exaggerate her skills of snoop.

If Lillie nodded any harder her head would shake off and roll across the floor. "You can count on me to do what I can."

"Jake." His eyes widened and he looked at Lillie, as if to wonder why anyone would address him without adding her name first. "Would you know anything about Arty?"

He shook his head. "Nope. Can't say I do."

"Since he's new to the village, no one seems to know much about him. But we know for a fact he had an argument with Dan Swansey prior to his death."

Jake motioned to Lillie to jot that down. "Lillie and I will see what we can find out."

Lillie scratched down notes on the paper with enthusiasm.

Fred and Jessica sat on the edge of the sofa and stared at me with anticipatory glances.

I was stabbing in the dark with the request I had for them. "Do you have any way to discover what Barbara Swansey does for the military? If you don't, please don't worry. Maybe someone else here can find out."

Fred pulled his legs in and sat further back in the sofa. With that quick gesture he seemed to grow ten inches. "Maybe I can ring up some blokes from the base I know from the Hare, see what they migh' be able to tell me."

Guess his endless hours at the pub might come in handy after all.

"Thanks, Fred. The other thing I'm curious about is if she and Dan were actually husband and wife. When Jim and I visited her at her house there was no indication she was married to him or anyone else. It was odd."

Jessica threw her ring-fingered hand into the air. "I know some people from the base when I worked part-time cleaning the TLF. You know, the lodging facility. Le' me ask around, too."

Jessica cleaned the TLF?

They say the trade you do for a living is the last thing you do in your own home. I could certainly attest to this in Jessica's case. "I had no idea you cleaned."

Jim side-kicked me on the ankle.

I clarified. "I mean I had no idea you cleaned on the base."

She was undeterred. "Tha' was a long time ago. Long before you and Jim lived here, but I still have friends who work there. They'll know about Barbara."

Jessica rummaged around her small, rather overstuffed, handbag. "Looking for a pen," she mumbled and pulled out a stub of a pencil. "This'll do." She scrabbled through her bag again. Papers, tissues, cards, and other paraphernalia piled on the sofa by her side. She lifted her eyes and realized she was the center of attention. "Um, looking for something to write on."

Lillie tore out a sheet from her writing tablet and handed it to Jessica.

Jessica nodded at Lillie. "Thanks." Two red splotches dotted her cheeks.

This was no small exchange of pleasantries between two women. This was one small step for mankind and one giant leap for Lillie. Never before had Lillie even acknowledged Jessica's presence in a room, let alone offered to help her.

Perhaps our gathering would be more than a set of untrained sleuths trying their hand at solving some crimes. This gathering might become a neighborhood melting pot where prejudices and mistrust would melt away and neighbors could begin depending on each other.

Jessica and Fred made a list of people they could call.

Jim slanted his head toward me, nodded in their direction, and smiled. This was the first time we had seen Fred and Jessica work together as a team. Our endless hours of counseling with them were finally bearing fruit.

I directed my next issue to Walter, and pulled out the envelope with Dan Swansey's name on it—now in a protective sandwich bag—from the side pocket of my Cath Kidston. "I found this letter the same time I discovered the necktie under the bush when I was heading to Serenity's.

"I know it's probably illegal to have kept this and not give it to the police right away. But it was an accident. I didn't intentionally keep it." I lifted my purse to demonstrate a point. "I found it buried in the bottom of a handbag after we got home from the police station yesterday. I'm not trying to impede the police investigation in any way nor do I want to put you in a compromising position. I need to know what to do. I'm afraid if I hand it over they will arrest me straight away, and I'm worried what Chief Inspector O'Reilly will do to Jim and me. He seems to have a vendetta against us for some reason."

Walter took the envelope and spoke tenderly. "Mrs. Weathervane, you know I'll have to give this to the police."

"Please call me Dotty." I twisted my fingers and, as if seeing them for the first time, was aware of how they'd aged. "I know.

But I thought you would be the best person to give it to, and I know you'll do what is best."

Walter looked at Jim and me. "Thank you. Both. For trusting me. It means . . ." He cleared his throat with a deep gurgle. "Let's just say it's been a long time since I've felt needed."

The room became quiet.

Walter loosened the collar along his neck with a sweep of his index finger. "It's nice to be a part of something worthwhile. Thanks."

Could be why he was drinking so much at the pub. He's lonely.

Jim said, "Walter, we trust you. You gave me some good advice the other day about the window and insurance. I'm sure you can handle this too."

Walter gave a nod. "I promise to do everything I can, within legal boundaries, of course. You've always been kind to me whenever I've seen you around the village, and I know without a doubt you don't have anything to do with these murders." He placed the envelope, still ensconced in the sandwich bag, in the middle of his notebook.

I eyed his notebook. "I know the envelope is addressed to Dan Swansey, but it might not have anything to do with his death or Amy Miser. Right?"

"I'm hoping with my connections I might be able to find out who sent the letter. But I want to be careful not to withhold any evidence. The police will need to have this and decide if it has any ties with the murders."

Kate straightened her skirt with a swish of her manicured fingers and touched her hair. "Seems I'm the only one you haven't assigned anything yet. So what can I do?"

I turned in her direction. "I'm hoping you can help me discover who broke our front window. Plus, I want to find out who's been calling our home and hanging up. It's happened a couple of times now."

"Is that all?"

"For now. If we can find out the answer to these two things it will give Jim and me peace of mind. They probably don't have anything to do with the murders but we can't be sure."

Jim stood. "Well, thank you for coming—"

"Jim," I snapped.

"What?"

"Don't be rude."

Everyone snickered. They knew Jim's passion for pansies and that he was probably itching to head outside, the trowel and gloves sitting at his feet a pretty good clue.

I stood and faced him. "We aren't finished."

"What more is there?" The questioning eyebrows rose.

"I thought we'd give ourselves a name or something."

Walter cleared his throat.

I softened my tone. "Maybe a secret handshake, like in the movies." I turned from Jim and included everyone. "Something only the eight of us know."

"Dotty."

"Maybe a secret code of some sort."

"Dotty." He tapped my shoulder.

I ignored him. "Let's decide what our name might be. Figure out where we want to meet next. When we get together we can bring each other up to speed on what we've found out."

"Dotty."

I spun back to him, fists on hips, ready to slug. "What?"

"I have an idea."

"You do?" My eyebrow went up. They say the longer a couple is married, the more like each other they become. I forced the eyebrow down.

Everyone snickered again.

Like the "pomp and circumstance" announcing the birth of a child, Jim's chest expanded and he clapped his hands. "Let's call ourselves the Crime Catchers."

The play on the name *Crime Stoppers*—a British television series in the same vein as *America's Most Wanted*—was quite clever.

"Love it." Lillie popped up. "Don't you, Jake?" She pulled him up by the elbow.

"Yes, dear."

"Ideal name, Jim." Walter stood, pulled in his stomach, and puffed out his chest.

"Superb idea, Jim," Kate sang, as she rose from her chair.

She and Walter exchanged glances. He smiled at her, a glimmer in his eyes. Could they have anything in common? And here I thought spinster Pauline would be the perfect match for him.

Did Kate just blush?

"Gotta agree." Fred stood with Jessica, stretched his elongated hand out, and shook Jim's.

"Dotty?" Jim said.

"What?"

"Aren't you going to say anything?"

"I'm speechless."

Jim wrapped his arm around my shoulder. "Been thinking about it ever since you had the idea to ask everyone over."

"But—"

"I know, I told you I didn't want to get involved."

"Right."

"You convinced me we had to do something, and these friends will help get us through this mess." He squeezed me.

"The Crime Catchers it is. We will stop at nothing to catch whoever has done these crimes."

As if making a toast, everyone raised their hands in unison and shouted together, "Hear, hear."

With that Jim ended our first meeting.

Everyone had an assignment and there was no time to waste. There were two murders to be solved, Barbara's identity to be uncovered, and a mysterious letter to deliver to the police. A new ad hoc detective agency was born, and I expected the killers wouldn't know what hit them.

Plus, Kate and I needed to have a quiet conversation about Walter in Molly's Tea Leaf before too long. Perhaps she didn't know what had hit her either.

Chapter Twenty-Nine

The Crime Catchers.

I jotted the words down on a slip of used paper buried under *Break* magazines spread on the kitchen countertop. I stacked the magazines into a haphazard pile and slid them aside. There were recipes I wanted to cut from them and try out. Jamie Oliver's mackerel salad and tiramisu dessert were two I had in mind for the spring garden party I was still planning—unbeknownst to Jim, of course. The magazines had tripled over the past few weeks, but my commitment to copying down recipes and cutting out photos was lacking.

Who would have guessed Walter and Kate? I chuckled, and wrote out a list of things to do:

First, set a date for follow-on meeting.

With the excitement of Jim naming our group, I had forgotten to settle on a date and time for our next get-together.

Second, where to meet? Hare and Hound? Make reservations.

It was great having everyone at our house, but it might be good to vary our routine. If we met at the pub for lunch it would appear more natural than perceived clandestine meetings with drawn shades. Good excuse to eat out too.

Third, go to the shop and speak with Jon or Carole—or whoever was manning the counter.

Their shop was a hubbub of news and activity, and I would be an inept detective if I didn't hit such a viable source of information.

While I made the list, Jim checked online about options on the cost of having the window fixed. He was following up on the repairman's estimate and realized the pre-bill we received was overpriced. It seemed the repairman was trying to gouge the insurance company.

Bliiiing.

"East Lark, 58 1808."

Two bursts of air. The obnoxious phone bandit who kept harassing me was at it again.

"Stop bothering us." I slammed down the receiver.

The police had telephoned after everyone had left, and confirmed others in the village were having trouble with similar prank phone calls. They assured us it was probably not tied to the murders or our broken window—a huge relief.

At least this was one less puzzle piece to be solved. Now I needed to figure out who threw the thing into our window.

With my list complete, I cut and clipped recipes from *Break* and tossed out the remaining sections of magazines.

I stretched and yawned. *That's enough for today.* "Want to go to the pub for a meal?"

"Nope." Jim grabbed his garden boots and slipped them on, computer business obviously finished.

"Didn't think so," I spoke to myself as he stepped out the back door.

Jim headed to the corner patch to continue repairing the hedge. His tattered green shirt was no longer the preferred dress as the weather had warmed. Instead, a torn short-sleeved tee would be the uniform of the day. At least he remembered his cap even though the day was waning.

The freezer held nothing that cried out "cook me, please." Not a word from anything, including the meat. The frozen pork chops kept "silent as a lamb."

Takeaway from the fish and chip shop, snuggled between Serenity and the village shop, was the perfect thing to satisfy any desire not to cook—although not included in the *Biggest Loser* contest by any means.

I grabbed my bag, stuck my head out the door, and shouted to Jim, "I'll be back soon."

A quick trip there and back, and entering the kitchen I plunked malt vinegar and sea salt on the table with the paper-wrapped, oil-saturated cod and chips.

The national anthem played over the speaker system.

Jim came inside.

The fish was quickly eaten and the leftover stack of chips tossed. Chips—French fries—were great when still hot from their oil dunk, but became soggy sticks of fat once cooled. I loved my culinary experiences but there were some things even I wasn't willing to compromise.

I stacked the dishes and piled the magazines. Tools stood in the corner implying the evil magician had been hanging around once more.

After my quick pick-up, I rang the Hare and Hound and made reservations for the Crime Catchers to meet in one week's time.

Lewis rerun and Jim's lip puffing as he slouched on the leather chair, his head dangling at a cock-eyed slant, was a comforting finale to a successful day.

For some reason I was sure tomorrow was going to be a turning point in solving the crimes in our village. Looked like we wouldn't need Lewis's help after all.

Chapter Thirty

Purchasing a newspaper was an ideal reason to go and query Jon and others in the shop for the latest news on village happenings. The special newspaper deal was over and no longer delivered at home. I jotted a note for myself to go immediately after breakfast.

I opened the kitchen French doors leading to the garden to let in warm morning air. Steam rose from the concrete, rainwater vaporizing from the sun's heat.

Sampson's pigsty cleaning had been finished, and the slight breeze brought in the aroma of newly birthed lilac instead. Jim had mowed the patch of green grass in the garden and scissor-clipped around the edges.

Ideal weather conditions promoted lazy behavior, so Jim and I lingered over breakfast, and Jim scanned yesterday's headlines. BBC Three played in the background.

"The garden looks wonderful."

The paper bobbed.

I crunched muesli bathed in yogurt.

"Think I lost a few pounds."

Jim and I had decided we needed to lose some weight. We cut out certain foods from our diet. An all-time favorite—bread in any shape or size—was a major item deleted along with any form of cheese.

Jim spoke through the day-old page, "Dot, we just started our diet yesterday."

I moaned, "Has it only been twenty-four hours?"

The paper nodded.

"Not sure I'm going to last."

The paper dropped. "It was your idea in the first place." Up the paper went.

When a couple retired and a husband stayed home more, conversations could either stimulate their relationship or put a big damper on its becoming a hot romance ever again. Dieting was one of those topics best left alone if hot romance was what they sought.

I tried a different subject. "I decided on the sofa I want."

The dancing paper shuffled, and I quit talking.

+ + +

After breakfast, I replaced the Cath Kidston purse and switched back to the vivid lemon-lime handbag. Odd papers were left in each one. I didn't have time to read every receipt or buried note found in them.

I tapped on the kitchen window. "I'm heading to the shop."

Jim was immersed in spindly weeds. He lifted his head and wiped his brow.

I stepped through the open doors. "Jim."

A robin scooted into a bush.

"I'm going to the shop to get the paper and a few other things."

He waved backhandedly, reaching up to trim dried leaves and wayward branches.

I was never certain if he heard me or not.

After a quick look in the mirror and a swipe of lipstick along thinning lips, I closed the front door. People said one's nose gets bigger and lips get thinner with age. Why couldn't it be the other way around? I would love to have Angelina Jolie lips and a Keira Knightley nose.

As I stepped out, I glanced across the street at the work still going on at the village hall.

The temporary fencing had partially fallen down. The work seemed to be taking longer than expected. But the pavement was tarred, PVC windows replaced, and roof repaired with adobe-colored tiles. In the center of the roof, three new blocks of aluminum-framed solar panels glistened in the bright sunlight.

Wonder if they ever fixed the broken lock Jonesy told us about.

I strolled past the postage-sized gardens and stopped to watch a horse canter past. The black-as-night beast had a lengthy stride. The rider wore a fluorescent pink helmet and matching leggings. Guess you can get away with wearing a Jane Fonda sixties outfit when you aren't more than thirteen.

Jon had rearranged everything in the shop. I grabbed a red-handled basket and went on a scavenger hunt for the few items on my list.

Morris was stocking milk in the shop's small refrigerator. "Things sure are strange around here these days."

Jon nodded as he placed Dunhill cigarette packs in their designated slots above the cash register. "Ever since that Swansey couple arrived we've had nothing but trouble."

I stepped closer.

"Not sure it's their fault." Morris thrust another bottle in the cooler.

"All I can say is—"

They both saw me and stopped.

"Good morning, Jon, Morris." I placed salt and vinegar crisps into the basket, along with the newspaper.

Morris's ruby face brightened, and he tapped his cap. "Hi ya."

Jon said, "Morning. What can I get you, Mrs. Weathervane?"

"Gossip." I chuckled.

He shook his head and placed another pack of cigarettes in a slot. "Can't say we've heard anything new."

"Now that's a shame. Guess I'll just pay for these few things. I need to get home. The repairman is supposed to fix the window sometime today."

"Sorry to hear what happened to your house." Jon put the last packet of Dunhill into place. "And sorry I can't help with any gossip." He gave me change from a ten-pound note.

Morris and I left the shop at the same time.

His truck, overloaded with things other than milk, stood curbside. He sold bread, crisps, and candy, and was a proverbial shop on wheels.

He tapped his cap once more and took off. Slowly—as milk trucks were generally prone to do.

Vivian approached the store using a ladies' walking cane. Her woolen skirt and sweater made me break out in a sweat. Women of her generation wouldn't be caught dead in a pair of slacks, never mind shorts.

We waved and went our separate ways.

Cobalt blue skies held lengthened contrails, white wisps dispersing over the horizon like feathers on an old-fashioned quill pen.

I stopped and plucked dead heads off Erika's plants along her stone wall. Weeds spiked through the pebbled walkway leading to the front door.

It was an ideal spring day. Perfect, in fact.

I turned the corner.

In front of our house sat an ambulance, and the emergency medical team carried Jim on a stretcher.

My purse slapped the pavement. "What's happened?" I screamed, running to the vehicle with flashing lights and opened rear end.

One of the medics came toward me. "Mrs. Weathervane? Please calm down."

He didn't realize the impossibility of that statement.

"What's happened to him?"

Jim's dimmed blue eyes blinked questioningly. His gray face and raspy breath through the oxygen mask frightened me. I cried and clasped the white sheet covering his torso.

The medic said, "You're welcome to ride in the ambulance with us and I'll explain along the way."

Time slowed as I ran back for my handbag, climbed into the boxed vehicle, and the door whammed shut.

As the ambulance sped down East Lark's twisted lanes toward the nearest hospital, I tipped this way and that with the ninety-degree turns.

One paramedic spoke, but sounded as if he talked underwater. "Your husband will be fine."

"But what happened? He was okay when I went to the shop. Did someone hurt him?" Question slinging increased under pressure.

Another paramedic efficiently handled the equipment and monitored Jim's vitals in spite of the speed and curves. "Apparently a repairman was coming to your house."

Sirens sounds were deafening. "Yes, a window repairman."

The first medic wrapped wiring around a stand, tucked a white sheet tighter around Jim's body, and draped a gray woolen blanket on his midsection. "When no one answered, the repairman went around back to see if anyone was in the garden. And it's a good thing he did."

"But what happened?" I rubbed Jim's cheek with the backside of my shaking hand.

Medical people were trained to speak deliberate. They can tell you your world is collapsing with the monotone voice of a salesperson selling electronic gadgets. "The repairman found him. Could be your husband fainted with the increased heat, or perhaps he's gotten dehydrated. But we need to be sure it's nothing more."

"Do you think someone could have tried to hurt him?"

"The doctor will need to do further tests, so let's just wait and see."

"Could he have had a stroke or something more serious?"

"Mrs. Weathervane." Tap, tap on my knee. "We'll have to wait and see."

It was no longer the perfect day. In fact, it was one of the worst days of my life.

Chapter Thirty-One

The house was quieter than St. Peter's church on a Friday night. I set my bag gently on the kitchen counter.

It was decided Jim would spend the night in the hospital. After many years of military life, I was used to him being gone. But after his retirement, I was also used to warming my cold feet on his back and watching him puff his lips until he fell into a deep sleep.

The whistling tarp over the broken living room window no longer sounded like musical accompaniment. Now it came closer to *The Addams Family*'s eerie mansion. I closed the living room door and headed upstairs. Smells of hospital disinfectant clung to my clothes so I tossed the lot into the overflowing hamper.

Numbers on the bedside clock flipped endlessly as I tossed and turned, and thoughts of Jim made sleep elusive.

05:00. I descended the stairs, flicked on the coffeepot, and turned on the radio for company. In spite of yesterday's soaring heat, this morning the sound of pitter-patter tapped on the window. The announcer had predicted early showers, sun later in the day.

Retirement was supposed to offer lazy days of sleeping in, holidays on the beach, and long strolls along the promenade—not trips to the hospital, sleepless nights, and worry-filled days. Forget retirement.

Bliiiing.

"East Lark, 58 1808."

"Did I call too early? Is Jim in the hospital? Erika was at the shop and saw the ambulance at your house with Jim being put inside. Why didn't you call me? Should I come over? Do you want me to do something?" Kate took a deep breath.

"I was already awake, and yes, Jim's in the hospital. It was too late to call you last night. There really isn't anything you can . . ." I lost composure and sobbed. "Oh, Kate." I put my hands together, trying to make them stop shaking. The phone rattled with the effort.

Inhale. Exhale. "What am I going to do? They will be taking more tests today, but he looked so sad and pathetic last night. All he did was suck on ice chips and sleep."

"I'll be right over." Kate hung up.

Ten minutes later she stood at the back door with a plate of scones and homemade jam tucked into a basket, a red-checked cloth draped over its side. She could have been a perfect stand-in for Little Red Riding Hood in her wellies and Burberry raincoat, a hood draped over her hair.

Kate hung her coat on the hallway hook and followed me to the kitchen. "The best thing we can do is indulge." She steered me to a chair, started the kettle, and set the table. "I'll drive you back to the hospital so you can be with Jim. I won't leave unless you ask me to."

Kate tipped my cold coffee into the dished-filled sink and refilled my Queen Elizabeth mug with hot tea.

The coffee cup reminded me of the many times Jim and I had sat in the kitchen over a relaxing breakfast. I began to cry again.

Kate reached across the table and patted my arm. "There, there, Dotty. What are they saying happened to Jim?"

"They're not sure." I used a hanky to wipe my face.

"No one tried to hurt him, did they?"

"That's the first question I asked."

The hot tea had a calming effect. Plus, I wouldn't have a stroke with a strong cup of *PG Tips* swimming through my veins—at least that's what they said in *Break.* "I was only gone to the shop for a few minutes, and when I got home they were loading him into the ambulance."

Kate pushed open the kitchen curtains, and daylight burst into the room. "Somehow things always seem to be less threatening in the light than in the dark. Don't you agree?"

I sniffled and stopped the tears. "They said the window repairman found Jim and called 999. But anyone could have gone into the garden before the repairman arrived."

"Who would want to hurt Jim?" Kate gazed out the window.

"I'm not sure. But do you think it could be related to the murders and him finding the knife in our garden?"

She turned toward me, a worried look making her normally soft face scrunch with fine lines. "Dotty, what are you going to do if someone did try and hurt him? You two need to be careful. I wouldn't want anything to happen to either of you."

I slapped the table with my palms and stood up. "I'll tell you one thing, if anyone has tried to hurt my Jim, they'll have to answer to me."

"Now that's my friend Dotty Weathervane speaking." Kate, her blue eyes blazing, came to me, held my forearms, and looked me in the eyes. "Why don't you get yourself dressed? We'll head to the hospital and see what they've found out and how Jim is doing. We might be wrong about someone hurting him, but if anyone has, they will have to answer to the both of us."

Her perfume was a welcome reprieve from the disinfectant still lingering in my nostrils from yesterday when I'd watched Jim being poked and prodded, and had felt completely helpless. "Thanks, Kate." Friends were the needed balm on a person's wounded heart.

Chapter Thirty-Two

I pulled the thermometer from Jim's mouth and tucked in the bedcovers. "Can I get you anything?"

"You've asked me the same thing at least fifteen times since I came home. And I've only been here ten minutes."

"I wanted to be sure you don't need anything before I go back downstairs."

"I promise to tell you if I do." He rolled into a fetal position and closed his eyes.

Gently, I touched his forehead one more time, pulled down the shade, flipped off the bedroom light, and shut the door.

The glow of the clock's numbers caught my attention: 2:45.

Several hours had passed since lunchtime and my stomach growled to remind me it was on empty.

"How is he?" Kate asked as I walked into the kitchen.

Sigh. "Tired."

"You look tired too."

"It's been a long thirty-six hours." I finger-combed my hair. When was the last time I did anything with this unruly mess of gray and white locks? Guess I could be called the Lock Mess Monster. "I couldn't have gotten through this without you, Kate. Thank you."

I wrapped an apron around my waist and turned on the kitchen taps. After pouring Fairy Liquid into the sink, adding a stack of dishes piled from days of neglect, I snapped on my rubber gloves. Retail therapy was one way of relieving stress, but stress was also another means by which I could get the house in order.

"You've been so kind, Kate. I can never repay you for everything you've done." Mist filled my eyes, making it difficult to see if all the caked-on leftovers stuck on the pot were gone. I placed it on the draining board.

DYING TO EAT AT THE PUB

Kate leaned on the counter as I began removing grime off a platter. "You would do the same for me." She straightened and touched her hair. How was it her hair was always so neat, and I couldn't keep a single strand of mine in place?

"Don't be so sure." I smiled. "Think about it. You brought the scones this morning. Took me to the hospital and brought Jim and me back home. That's going above and beyond the call of friendship duty." I gave her a half salute with a dripping hand. "Not sure I'm that good of a friend." I chuckled and plunged my hands back into the sudsy water.

Kate grabbed a tea towel from the drawer and began drying. "I'm glad he's home and getting better."

Leaning my wet hands on the sink, I stopped. "I'm thankful he was only dehydrated from the heat and no one had tried to hurt him. With everything else that's happened, I was sure someone had done something to him."

I wiped my hands on a towel and took the other one from Kate. "Thanks. You've done enough for me already."

We hugged for a moment and she headed toward the door.

Bliiiing

"Hi, Lillie." I winked at Kate knowingly.

Lillie had taken longer to call than normal. I actually found myself worrying about her as she's usually ahead of the game when it comes to playing busybody.

Kate mouthed, "Let me know if you need anything."

I placed my hand over the mouthpiece and whispered, "Will do."

"Dotty. Are you there? Are you and Jim okay? I heard what happened. I'm so sorry I didn't call sooner. Jake and I were away." Zing. Zing. Lillie's speaking speed was even faster than normal.

"I'm fine. Jim's fine." I knew deep down she meant well. "He got a little dehydrated, that's all. By the way, I was going to call you."

"You were?" She gasped as if surprised.

"The Crime Catchers will have their next meeting on Monday at the Hare and Hound. I've made reservations for twelve o'clock. Could you call the others and let them know?"

"Of course, I would be happy to."

"Lillie?" She had hung up.

Chapter Thirty-Three

The paper shuffled.

"Now don't get upset." I snickered.

Down the paper went.

"Glad you're home again, Jim." I smiled.

"Me too." Up the paper went.

It was a new day, house totally cleaned, Jim home, and routine back to normal. What more could I want? Perhaps the window repaired. Sofa bought. Murders solved. There was much to do, but for the moment BBC Three playing softly, the paper swishing, and me humming Paul Simon's "Homeward Bound" meant life was indeed good.

Jim dropped the paper.

I stopped humming.

Up the paper went.

Fruit bowl and a thin slice of cheese sat pathetically on my plate. "How long do you think I need to be on a diet to officially be named a 'big loser'? Besides, who wants to be known as a 'loser' anyway?" I swallowed a strawberry.

The flagpoled paper went down. "Dotty, why are you torturing yourself?"

"My clothes are too tight and I want to lose some weight."

Up the paper went.

Jim knew better than to say anything. If he agreed, he would be in big trouble. If he disagreed I knew he'd be lying, and he would still be in trouble. There are times a man is better off keeping quiet, not moving, and staying behind the paper. After all these years of marriage he knew perfectly well this was one of those times.

One last sip of Earl Grey and Jim was on his feet. He crumpled the paper and thrust it into the recycling bag.

"And where do you think you're going, Mr. Weathervane?"

"Outside." He grabbed his work gloves and headed toward the door.

I jumped and played linebacker, tackling him around the waist before he had a chance to even touch the doorknob. "Not a chance."

"But my plants have missed me."

I took his gloves, handed him his gardening book, and gently guided him to the living room and his favorite chair. "One more day inside. Doctor's orders."

He glanced over my shoulder at the back door. "I want them to know I'm home and okay, that's all."

"There'll be plenty of time for you to go out and dig in the dirt. I don't want anything more to happen to you. You might drive me mad as mud, but I want several more years to pay you back."

He sat. "But Dot . . ." I touched his brow with my lips.

He placed his legs on the ottoman, closed his eyes, and his lips started puffing.

Sigh. All was truly well with the world.

Chapter Thirty-Four

It was almost time:

Time to meet with the village sleuths: Fred and Jessica, Lillie and Jake, Walter and Kate.

And it was time to pursue the hunt for the killers of Dan Swansey and Amy Miser, to get Police Constable Jones and Chief Inspector O'Reilly off our backs, and to find out who broke our front window.

Lillie confirmed everyone would be at the pub on Monday for lunch. I was certainly going to miss the excuse to eat out when the hubbub was over and the murderer or murderers locked behind bars. In the meantime, I was going to take every advantage to visit the Hare and Hound and get my fish and chips soaked in vinegar whenever I could.

In the meantime, the window repairman had begun working.

Jim was back to his gardening and I was back to my planning:

First, plan the agenda for the next Crime Catchers meeting in two days. Although most of the details were taken care of by now.

Second, plans for the soon-to-be surprise garden party for Jim. I finally had the recipes I needed and began a list of required ingredients. The garden was beautiful, and for the first time ever, Jim was successful in establishing his bedding plants and borders.

Finally, I planned on buying the sofa for our living room today.

I put the list for the Crime Catchers and garden party away.

A quick change of handbags and clothes and I was ready to head to Harvey's furniture store.

"Jim? Where are you?"

I looked in the garden. He wanted to get back to pruning sooner than he should, and I didn't have the heart to say no any longer.

There was no sign of him.

I stuck my head into the living room. The window was coming along and would soon be finished. The glass was reinstalled but the frame needed a fresh coat of paint. Every step took time. But before long we would forget the window breaking ever happened and my whistling companion would be gone forever.

"Jim?" I started to panic. It seemed I wasn't quite over his episode in the hospital.

I went back to the garden.

"Jim?" My voice squeaked.

His head poked out from behind the hedge. "Looking for me?"

"You gave me a start." I caught my breath. "What in the world are you doing behind there?" My voice was tinged with anger.

"Looking for weapons." He smiled. "Only kidding."

Did he just snort?

What did they do to him at the hospital? Insert a funny bone?

"You should not be overdoing it."

He clapped his gloved hands and dirt flew around his face. "I know, doctor's orders. Or would that be Dotty's orders?" *Snort.* A smirk stretched across his face. "I needed to finish up back here, and pretty soon the hedge will be almost new again."

They must have dripped some words through the hospital IV and into his vocal bank account, too. He seemed to talk more since he'd come home. Could it be the drugs? Generally, they make folks sluggish and quiet. With Jim they had the opposite effect.

"Just wanted you to know I'm heading to Harvey's. Their sale is over tomorrow."

The eyebrow rose. "Do you want me to come with you?"

Something is definitely wrong here.

I couldn't remember the last time Jim offered to go shopping with me. If this kept up, I was calling the doctor or taking him back to the hospital myself. Jim might drive me crazy but I was used to him, and I didn't know what to do with the new guy living under the same roof with me.

"No. I'll be back shortly so don't overdo it out here. Please. I'll worry about you the whole time I'm gone unless you promise you'll take it easy."

"Fine."

That was more like it.

+ + +

Thump da-de thump. I hit several curbs, but two pheasants kept their lives.

I was bound and determined to get a handle on this driving thing—even if it took me the rest of my life. And there were fewer "rest of my lifetimes" to get it right.

Harvey's choices were numerous. The newspaper insert gave no indication how large the place was and how many options I would have. I was thankful I took the time to cut out some photos and had a pretty good idea what I was looking for. Plus, I knew exactly how much I could spend. Both these things kept the search to a minimum, and I was able to decide quickly on a brown leather, double-thick style known as Victoria. The pulled buttons on the back and curled arms would match our two seats perfectly.

Satisfied, I returned home and found Jim resting in the living room with a stack of DIY books from the local library that I had picked up for him while he was in the hospital.

BBC Three played softly in the kitchen as I fixed leftovers for dinner.

We had an early night. Jim fell asleep in front of the telly while I picked up and straightened the kitchen.

I directed Jim up to bed, flicked off the coffee pot, lights, and radio, and got ready for a good night's sleep.

Chapter Thirty-Five

04:12. So much for a good night's sleep.

My mind flipped and flopped like a fish slapping back and forth on a sandy beach trying to reach water.

Jim's curled form lay next to me.

04:15. Had there really been two murders in the village? Or was it some horrible mistake? Was Dan Swansey thrown into a dumpster at the pub, stabbed with a bowie knife?

04:20. Amy Miser—killed with a tie and nylons—was she someone Dan knew and for some unknown reason they both had to die? Nothing seemed to be resolved, and like the broken window, I hoped things could be figured out quickly and soon be forgotten.

04:24. There were moments in life when reality felt like a dream, and dreams felt like reality. The murders seemed to be a horrific nightmare, and I would wake up in the morning to a quiet and calm home, albeit still not *Southern Living* standards.

I closed my eyes and finally drifted off to sleep.

Blackness. So thick I couldn't see. Anything. Including my hand in front of my face. I was running, panting. Heard my footsteps on the tarmac, smacking bare feet. Trying to escape. I ran into the village hall, slammed the door shut, slithered down, and hid. Footsteps came toward me. Someone jiggled the handle and pushed against the locked door. I stifled a scream by putting my fist into my mouth and biting into the skin. I peered through the keyhole and in the dim light of a swinging bulb saw someone. Who was it? Jake? Could it possibly be him? Where was Lillie? Whoever it was, the person left. I relaxed my shoulders and took my hand away. Someone clapped a hand over my mouth, pulled me to the floor, and started shaking me.

"Dotty, Dotty."

Jim's voice came from a distance, and I screamed, "Help. Help me." The vise grip on my mouth was gone, and I was sitting straight, sweat drenched, Jim shaking my shoulder.

"Dotty, it's okay. You were having a bad dream."

I flung myself into his arms and wept.

The murders *were* real, the dream a frightening reminder there was someone out there who murdered two people and for some reason was trying their best to put the blame on Jim and me.

Jim served me coffee in bed in my Queen mug. As I caught my reflection in the drink, I nearly dropped the thing. It had been a long night. My java mirror had just proved it.

"Yikes."

"Are you okay, Dotty?" He touched my brow.

"Yes, just scared myself, that's all."

He shook his head. "Dot, this is why—"

"I know, I know. This is why you didn't want me to get involved."

He sat beside me on the bed, rabbit-eared hair poking sideways. "Dotty, once this mess is cleared up, let's go away for a few days. We both could use it."

Several meals at the pub and perhaps a potential vacation. Were the murders worth these special treats? I wasn't so sure.

+ + +

Daylight put darkness into perspective and did the same with dreams.

I got up and began making the bed; flicked the emerald-colored sheets and straightened the wrinkles, tucked in the corners with hospital precision, pulled the pale green striped coverlet up, and fluffed the pillows.

Pausing to consider the nightmarish dream with Jake stalking me, I wondered about him as a possible suspect. Could he have something to do with these crimes?

I shook my head and tossed two decorative pillows on the bed.

Jake was about as capable as Fred in hurting anyone. Even less so. His mousy demeanor and "yes, dear" replies to Lillie indicated a weak-minded man. Yet Ed Gein, psycho killer, was considered harmless by his neighbors too, wasn't he?

Maybe Lillie's overbearing personality was more than Jake could take.

I opened the bedroom window and leaned on the sill. The children's playground across the street next to the village hall always provided a heart-lifting scene. Every afternoon uniform-clad youngsters from the local school climbed on slides, swung madly, or spun on the "wheel." *If I tried any of those gadgets I wouldn't be able to stand for a week.*

Right now the playground area was as quiet as a crypt and was closed during the hall's renovation, but was expected to open soon. Flyers posted throughout the village boasted a reopening celebration of both places in ten days' time. Bales of fencing and wooden slats sat precariously around the building and playground, so the workers had plenty to clean up before the opening due date.

I inhaled and closed my eyes.

The fresh air floating through the open window brought back a time when I had picked something up from the Bakersfield farm last winter, and Lillie had been acting very foolishly toward Jake.

Jake had offered ground salt to Jim and me for our driveway, to help with icy patches formed on sunless areas. I'd gone there to pick it up.

+ + +

I'd arrived to find Jake hunched over a massive tractor's engine, wellies covered in frozen mud chunks. Icicles dripped from the machinery and small pools of melted snow under his feet were bound to freeze again in the night.

"Can you believe him, Dotty?" Lillie stood in the doorway, nodded toward Jake, and spoke loud enough for him to hear.

Jake lifted his head and hit it on the tractor frame. "Blast." He rubbed his head with stiffened fingers. "I'll put the salt in your boot, Dotty." Meaning the trunk of the car, of course.

Lillie frowned and wrinkled her nose as if smelling rotting flesh, and said to him, "You are such a sight."

Lillie had invited me in, blustery air whisking through the opened front door. We stepped into the front hall, and she insisted I have a cup of coffee or tea.

"I don't have the time."

"Nonsense. There's always time," she dictated.

Before closing the door, she said to Jake, "Why do you have to get so dirty? Your wellies are a disgrace." She shut the door as Jake tossed the bag of salt into the car. "Tsk, he embarrasses me sometimes, Dotty. Why can't he be neater? Did you see the mess out there? I've been at him for weeks to clean up the filth piling around the shed. It's as if he totally ignores me."

I should have known better and not said a word. "I guess I expect a farmer to get dirty."

"Dotty." The tone resembled a parent to a child. "Of course a farmer gets dirty. But Jake somehow makes everything difficult, and I can't get him to see why he upsets me so much."

I couldn't see why he upset her so much either. Whenever I saw him, Jake was either working very hard or trying to placate his very demanding wife.

Lillie the martyr lamented, "If you only knew what I have to put up with." A huge sigh came from her heaving chest.

Why couldn't I get the idea out of my head Jake was the one putting up with someone and something?

"Are you sure you aren't being too hard on him?" I hoped to open Lillie's eyes to appreciate Jake's finer points. "He works hard for you and your sons. Farming is not easy. You more than anyone should know that."

"My father never looked like that when he ran our farm," she spouted over her teacup, nodding her head toward the door.

So that's what this was all about. Daddy comparison. One of the biggest mistakes a wife can make is to expect her husband to be like her father.

"Lillie, try and be nice to Jake. You might see him change if you'll only try harder."

"Nice? I'm nice. And you know me, Dotty. I do mean well." She sipped and looked in the distance, the gaze of an angel with halo hanging overhead.

Yep, I'd forgotten Lillie meant well no matter what she was doing.

Leaving the house and stepping into my car, I saw Jake once again under the tractor lift his head to look at Lillie standing in the doorway, as he waved goodbye to me. What was the meaning of his stare? Was that what unbridled anger looked like?

The entire drive home I was haunted by Jake's twisted face.

+ + +

I opened my eyes. The playground's bouncy frog rattled in the wind on its oversized spring. Jake's face stayed frozen in my mind.

The breeze coming in chilled my bones. I slammed the window shut, left the bedroom, and headed downstairs to begin the day.

Chapter Thirty-Six

The paper swished.

I pushed the button down on the toaster, stacked two Weetabix in a bowl, and soaked them with whole milk. The "biggest loser" contest was lost by me—at least for the moment. "Anything of interest in the news?"

"Nope."

"Do you want to see what sofa I ordered?" I flipped eggs in the pan.

"Nope." Next page turned. "Trust you."

The medicine obviously had worn off as Jim was back to his one-word answers.

I set the buttered toast and egg in front of him, poured my coffee, and sat. "How does it happen?"

Rustle. Rustle. Hand came around from the paper and bread disappeared behind the news like a magic trick.

I buttered my toast, added a spoon of homemade preserves on top, and began humming "Loves Me Like a Rock."

Down the paper went.

I offered him a Cheshire grin. "At least I didn't tell you not to get upset."

Up the paper went.

"Don't you want to know what I meant when I asked the question, 'How does it happen?'"

His head popped out from behind the paper, the questioning eyebrow raised, jaw working on toast, and a look of resignation sitting on his face. He swallowed the bread and started on the egg, eyes peering over his fork at me. "How does what happen, Dot?"

I outstretched both hands as if trying to sweep up the room with the brush of my arms. "This mess. Do you think an evil magician visited the kitchen during the night while I was tossing and turning and having wicked nightmares?"

"Not sure." Down the fork went, up went the paper.

I spoke into my cup, "Sure glad you're home." The words echoed with anger.

Down the paper went. "Me too." Jim stood, took a swallow of tea, grabbed his tools, and opened the door.

I snatched the paper and hunted for my glasses buried again under a pile of whatevers.

The cool air tickled up my legs. Felt like déjà vu.

"Dotty."

I lowered the paper.

Jim held the doorknob. "We might get upset with each other..." He switched his tools from one hand to the other, shuffled his feet in rhythm, his voice soft like a purring kitten. "But I worry about you. Like you worry about me. I'm sorry you had such a terrible dream last night. Believe me, I'll be glad when this is all over."

My heart melted like butter on hot toast. "Thanks, Jim." I spoke to the closed door.

+++

The whole ordeal would soon be over. I was sure of it.

Tomorrow was the big meeting at the Hare and Hound for the Crime Catchers.

After catching up with the headline news, I began reviewing notes from our previous get-together here at the house: Lillie finding out about Amy Miser, Jake asking around about Arty, Fred and Jessica looking into Barbara Swansey's job and marriage, Walter delivering the letter with Dan's name on it to the police, and Kate and me trying to figure out who broke our front window.

I was looking forward to what everyone had discovered. The suspense was killing me. To stem the tide of anticipation, I rang

Kate and asked her to meet me for tea. And perhaps she could help me figure out some clues about the window.

+++

Molly's Tea Leaf's back garden was open. Spring officially had arrived.

Kate and I sat on picnic-type chairs, with a tea tray of drinks placed on a slatted wooden table in front of us.

New potted plants hung over fencing posts, and an infant lemon tree took residence in a terracotta pot centered on the small patio. I only knew what it was because a small badge sitting in the potted dirt read "lemons." Fresh green sprouts peeked out from under the soil along the edging and would soon be bearing homegrown vegetables.

Mid-summer, the place would be filled with foliage and customers. Now it was fairly quiet and the sun had plenty of space to spread, so we both threw our heads back and absorbed sunrays on our faces like the new solar panels on the village hall roof.

A moment later, a slight shake of the fruit tree and thin cloud cover testified our sundrenched lounge in the garden would soon be coming to an end. Spring weather was predictably unpredictable.

After the waitress took our food order, I filled Kate in on my dream about Jake. "What do you think?"

She shook her head. "I can't see it. Jake's too nice."

"I can't see it either." I nodded in agreement. "So, what do you think about Walter?"

At that moment our desserts arrived and Kate exhaled a loud sigh of relief.

The waitress, a young gal with long legs stretching from under her skimpy black skirt, was the complete opposite of the other woman who worked there. They were as different as a pumpkin was from a carrot. The one woman resembled a pumpkin, this one a carrot.

The girl's burnt orange locks—straight from a hair-coloring box—were spiked, and looked like a bird of paradise flower. Her skin was so pale the striking difference between hairdo and flesh made her look anemic. She delivered our sweets—thick icing spiced cake for me and for Kate a sponge with fruit and cream—with little decorum, as if she were setting down a dog dish. The food was wonderful, the service questionable.

As soon as she left, Kate asked, "How's Jim?"

"Stop delaying."

"I don't know what you mean."

"Jim's fine. What about Walter?"

Kate put the cup to her mouth, covering a bright red blush rushing across her cheeks. "He's fine, I guess." She shrugged her shoulders.

"I think he was flirting with you during our meeting at my house."

"Dotty." She set her cup down. "It's been so long since a man paid attention to me I wouldn't know a flirt from a flit." She giggled.

I slid the fork through the thick cake and left it sitting on the edge of the plate. Then put my fingertips together in a prayer-like pose. "Why haven't you ever married? I've known you a long time, but never asked because I thought it wasn't my business."

"The house, the horses, and I guess life just seemed to take over. I was so busy I never had time to consider marriage, and before I knew it I was past my prime."

An image of Jim buried behind his morning paper popped in my mind. He'd be spitting bullets at me if he knew I was trying to be a matchmaker between Kate and Walter. But he didn't know and I certainly wouldn't be the one to tell him.

"You know, Kate, marriage can be hard, and wonderful, and sometimes both at the same time. But I can't imagine Jim not being here. And you are by no means past your prime."

"Dotty, you and Jim have something very, very special. I hope you realize how truly special it is."

"There are plenty of times I forget."

"Don't ever forget. Otherwise someone else might come along and snatch him from you." She winked and put her hand out, palm up. A few droplets landed on her opened hand. "Can we stop talking about marriage and Walter for now? We are a long way from that." She flicked the water in my direction.

"Of course. I wanted to ask you about our living room window anyway for the Crime Catchers meeting tomorrow. I need to come up with some ideas of who could have smashed it."

Our "carrot" waitress picked up our tray, dirty dishes, and crumbled serviettes, and slapped the bill upside down on the table. Kate snatched it. "My turn." She placed a ten-pound note on the table.

More drips started to fall. A drop of water hit my upturned face. "I need to have something to share, and I haven't figured out a thing. In fact, now that the window is repaired, it's like it never happened."

Rain pattered harder on the cement patio. I grabbed my umbrella and jacket. Kate grabbed hers. We dashed from the garden, through the restaurant, and out to our cars. Solutions to the breaking of our window went unanswered.

Chapter Thirty-Seven

I dashed inside the house through the front door.

Jim ran inside from the back garden.

The skies opened, as if every bit of water from heaven was let loose in order to refill the heavenly tanks.

Jim shook his clothing and smiled like a child who had a chance to play in a mud puddle with no one scolding him.

Kate was spot on. Jim was special. And right now, he was especially wet. But I didn't have the heart to reprimand him.

The rain continued through dinner, dishes, and the decision on what to watch on television.

Living room lights and SKY channel were turned on.

We settled into our chairs. As Jim hit the remote to change channels, the electricity flicked on and off, on, and then off—permanently.

The house was black—couldn't see the hand in front of my face darkness—exactly like my dream.

I yelped like a sick puppy.

"Dotty, what's wrong?"

"Did you hear that?" I whispered.

"I didn't hear a thing other than rain beating against the window. Sure glad it's fixed."

My heart palpitated as if I had finished a marathon. Which was hard to imagine—running a marathon, I mean. "Where are you?" I whispered.

No reply.

I squealed like a pig.

"Dotty, what's wrong now?"

"You didn't answer me."

"I was looking for some candles."

Jim struck a match and lit two tapers on the dining room silver-plated candelabra he had brought into the living room.

Menacing shadows moved along the wall as we made our way up the stairs, candelabra in his hand. I clung to his shirt as he guided us to the bedroom.

I would be extremely relieved when the village murders were solved and everything around me no longer seemed like a horror movie. Without a doubt another sleepless night awaited me.

Chapter Thirty-Eight

Even with little sleep, energy surged through my veins.

And energy surged through the electric wiring once more. Lights, camera, action. Everything was back to normal after a night of darkness and an overactive imagination keeping me awake.

"Morning, Dot." Jim planted himself on the chair and opened the paper.

"Good morning, Mister Sunshine." I pulled the kitchen curtains open and released the sun into the room. Remnants of last night's rain were long forgotten, other than a few puddles that still lingered in broken pockets on the brick patio.

On tiptoe, I stretched my arms as high as possible, bent at the waist, and raised my arms once more. The beaming rays rejuvenated me.

It was going to be a busy day.

The repairman would come to put the final coat of paint on the front window, and the meeting of the Crime Catchers was at noon.

Hot coffee steamed from my Queen mug.

I sat at the kitchen table, writing pad in hand, leopard glasses perched on the tip of my nose, and wracked my brain for ideas. I chewed the end of the pencil. Kate and I hadn't come up with a solution about who broke the front window when we met at Molly's Tea Leaf. And I needed something to share with the group. After all, I was the one who asked everyone to help us. The least I could do was answer my own question and set an example to the others on completing a job.

Tap. Tap. I drummed my fingertips on the table. "Sure wish I could figure this out."

The newspaper collapsed, then folded. "What are you trying to figure out?"

"You mean you heard that?"

"It's hard not to hear you chewing the pencil, grinding your teeth through the wood. I thought we had a chipmunk in the kitchen."

I stared at the pencil. A vampire-looking bite nearly cut the wood in two. "Sorry. I'm trying to figure out who could've broken our window and why."

"What have you come up with so far? Maybe I can help."

I looked around, glanced up at the ceiling, and scanned the room. Lifted the paper and looked under the table.

"What's the matter? What are you looking for?" Jim followed my path with his eyes.

"I wondered what alien ship landed here and dropped off a guy looking like my husband. Only this guy is interested in what I am doing and wants to help."

"Nice, Dot." Up the paper went.

I pulled the paper down in the center. "Only kidding. Of course I'd like your help. I've come up with a couple of possibilities."

He tapped my writing tablet with his forefinger. "Tell me what you've come up with."

"Well, it could have been an accident, someone coming from the Queen's Treat with one too many pints under their belt. They could've tossed something without meaning to. Jonesy's always been worried it might happen someday. Wonder where she was if it *was* a karaoke singer gone crazy? She's always been on the lookout. Of course the one time she isn't around, something like this happens." I stopped rambling and chewed the end of the pencil again.

"Okay, Dot. That's one idea." He pulled the pencil from my mouth. "What else do you think?"

"It could've been done on purpose. Someone trying to scare you and me, or worse, frame us for the murders by putting attention on us. Making sure we found the weapons. Then throwing something in the window to add to the police's suspicions." I brought the pencil toward my face. Jim's stare stopped me.

Jim pointed to my list. "Anything else?"

"Well? There is one other thing I've thought about."

"What?"

"It seems foolish."

"No idea is silly at this point, Dot."

I went to a kitchen drawer, dug around like a squirrel looking for a buried nut, and pulled out a golf ball.

Jim's questioning eyebrow rose. "Where did that come from?"

"I found three of these in the front garden. Put them in my bag and forgot about them until I cleaned out my last handbag. I couldn't figure out where they came from and I've been meaning to ask you."

Jim took the ball and spun it around in his palm. "Well, I'll be. Why didn't you mention this before?"

"With everything going on, I totally forgot." I sat and stared at the spinning ball. "When I cleaned up the kitchen and was putting things away I saw it again, there in the drawer." I pointed to the cupboard. "Do you think this could be the culprit? But where did it come from? Who would have hit a golf ball into the window? Why would someone hit a golf ball into *our* window?" My question slinging got out of hand.

Jim touched my forearm. "Wait a minute." He left the room, quickly returned, went to the counter, and turned the kettle on.

"Where did you go?"

"Shhh. Give me a sec. I'm thinking," He had restarted his Earl Grey ritual. In the many years we'd been married I had never seen Jim go through the Olympic tea-making routine twice in one morning. This was serious business.

"I'm happy to give more than a second, I'll give you the entire day if you figure out where this came from and if that's how the window was shattered."

He snapped his finger. "I've got it." The electric kettle screamed from steam, then popped off.

Chapter Thirty-Nine

"What? What have you got?"

"I think I've figured out what happened."

"Jim Weathervane, stop keeping me in suspense."

He brought his Earl Grey to the table. "Well, well, well." He sat and stared over my shoulder, a pensive look carved around his eyes and mouth. "We'll need to call Jonesy."

I grabbed Jim's hand. "Why?"

He put his face into his arm resting on the table.

I released his hand and held my head. "Oh, dear. Not again. You think this is connected with the murders, don't you?" My throat tightened and tear ducts began working.

Jim lifted his head. The grin spreading across his face was long enough to swing on. "Sorry, Dot. I didn't mean to alarm you. Just having a bit of fun." *Snort.*

"What are you talking about?" The hair on the back of my neck began to rise. "Do you mean to tell me we don't have to call Jonesy? That's not funny." I pushed back from the table.

"Oh, no. We still need to call her and say that we think we figured out who the culprit is. And for her to let O'Reilly know we had nothing to do with the breaking of the window. And it has absolutely nothing to do with the murders." He sipped his Earl Grey as if nothing had been amiss.

I slapped the table. "I don't understand."

Jim picked up the ball. This time he held it under his forefinger and spun it on the tabletop. "I am officially a Crime Catcher. This little guy indeed did the deed."

"How?"

"Well, it wasn't exactly him." Jim stopped the ball mid-spin and reached into his pocket. "This is the real window breaker." He opened his palm and offered another ball.

"Where did that come from?" I pulled the golf ball out of his hand.

"The living room."

"But the police looked everywhere."

"They didn't know to look in the one place where everything gets lost. Think about it, Dotty." He lined the two balls in a row.

"The sofa?"

"Of course."

I giggled, relaxed into the seat, and crossed my arms. "How many things have fallen into that space under the cushions where the fabric's torn? That's one of the reasons I wanted to replace it. But how did it end up in there?"

"I believe it's the neighborhood lad who hits golf balls on the green patch by the playground. Thinks he's Tiger Woods or something."

"I've never seen him."

"I've only caught him a couple of times and the last time I warned him the ball might go into someone's window if he wasn't careful. But I forgot about it until you showed me this. He and his brother have been troublesome at times with their shenanigans, but this is something we need to take to the next level. Their parents."

"He must have been out there in the middle of the night trying to hit the balls under the lamplight so he wouldn't get caught. No wonder it went through the window."

"Looks like we've solved one problem, don't you agree?"

I jumped up. "Yeah! That's such great news." I grabbed Jim by the neck and squeezed until he reached up and pulled my arms off. He was beginning to turn purple. "You did it. I can't wait to tell Jonesy so she can pass it on to that gorgeous god of an angry chief inspector. Going to call her now." I grabbed the phone.

Jim coughed—guess I squeezed harder than I thought. "Dot, it can wait a few more minutes. It's still early." He rubbed his neck to get the blood circulating again.

"I know it's early." I picked up the phone.

Jim shook his head and retreated behind the paper.

"Could I please speak to Police Constable Jones?"

The receptionist answered, "One minute, please. May I ask who's calling?"

"Mrs. Weathervane. Mrs. Dotty Weathervane. I'm sure she'll want to speak to me right away."

"Hold on, please." Classical strands played in the background over the phone. It felt like I was waiting for a bank manager or someone from a medical clinic, not the police station. I would have expected to hear Michael Jackson's "Thriller" or some other creepy-type music. "I'm sorry, Mrs. Weathervane, but PC Jones is currently unavailable. Can I have her return your call?"

"Yes. Please." They didn't know I had her personal cell number and could call her at a whim.

"Guess I won't worry about it right now."

"Told you it was too early and it could wait." Up the paper went.

+ + +

What I couldn't wait for was to get to the Hare and Hound and tell the others our news. The second meeting of the Crime Catchers was sure to be informative. Plus, it would give me direction on what our next steps should be as a group.

I stood at the open kitchen door. Jim's garden was truly looking spectacular. "It's time to get ready."

Jim looked over his shoulder. "For what?"

"The Crime Catchers meeting at the Hare and Hound. Remember? I told you we have a meeting there today."

"Oops, forgot. What time?"

"Reservations are at noon. But I want to go early to make sure I'm there before everyone else."

He glanced at his watch hidden under his left glove. "Dot, it's only nine-thirty. I have plenty of time." Down he went back to the dirt.

I headed upstairs to change bags and clothes, and put my notes together.

+ + +

An hour and a half later, I was back at the kitchen door wearing light brown slacks and a white and maroon top, carrying an enormous matching brown with maroon flecks handbag over my left arm. The bag was a find from a local charity shop.

Charity shops were introduced to Great Britain in the nineteenth century and each shop offers clothing, furniture, books, music, or kitchenware. My favorite shop, Age UK, on High Street next to Molly's Tea Leaf, offers a large selection of handbags—old and new. What more could one ask for than an inexpensive bag to add to one's collection? Surely one could never have enough bags to cram into a closet already jam-packed with them.

"Jim?"

He gave me a backhanded wave.

I stepped into the garden. "Jim!"

He stood and placed his hands on the backside of his hips, stretched backwards, and spun toward me at the waist. "Did you call me, Dot?"

Ugh. "I'm going to the pub."

He looked at his watch. "Dotty, it's only eleven o'clock. I still have plenty of time to get ready."

"Fine. Meet me there, okay?"

The Hare and Hound had their windows and doors wide open. The cross breeze was warm and pleasant. The darkened rooms were cheered by beams of light landing on tables and across the worn flowered rug. With the added natural daylight, scars appeared deeper on furniture and the mismatched chairs were unattractive. The pub would do well with an internal overhaul. Perhaps the workers at the village hall should come here next.

I waved to Roger, manning the bar. He pointed to an area in the back of the dining room. The man hardly spoke but was as efficient as Greenwich Mean Time.

A rectangular white placard on a table read "Reserved."

By rearranging the chairs, I ensured Kate and Walter would sit next to each other and directly across from me so I could watch the body language between them. Perhaps a little *coup de foudre* would happen before my very eyes.

Once I finished setting everything up, I paced the room. I couldn't wait to hear what they found out. Now was the appointed hour and the anticipation was killing me.

Chapter Forty

First to arrive: Lillie and Jake. Of course.

Jake was tidied up. His wellies were replaced with loafers, his hair was slicked back, and his cord pants with white open-collared shirt was an attractive combination. Maybe he finally decided to clean up after Lillie's constant haranguing about being such a dirty farmer.

Lillie carried her usual tapestry bag and Miss Marple hat, and she wore a frumpy grayish dress with uneven hemline. She looked tired, but she was her animated self and began talking before she even got near the table, her bag held tightly to her chest. "Wait until I tell you what I found out."

"Let's not share until everyone is here. Okay?" I entreated.

She nodded. Her authoritative voice kicked in. "Good plan, Dotty. I'm sure everyone will want to listen to what I found out about Amy Miser. In fact, wait until you hear I discovered—"

"Lillie. Please. Wait."

Jake pulled out a chair for her. She didn't acknowledge the gentlemanly gesture but sat and immediately opened her bag to begin a length of stitches on the sleeve of a sweater she was working on.

"By the way, where's Jim?" Lillie queried as her needles click-clacked.

"He'll be here shortly."

Fred and Jessica walked in. They were completely different in how they behaved toward each other. I'd have to get used to the new them. Jessica held Fred's arm and he walked as if he were leading the Queen to her throne. She beamed. "Fred's go' a job."

I managed to keep my jaw from dropping by rubbing my chin. "That's wonderful. I'm so pleased for you both. What's your new job, Fred?"

He looked down at Jessica as if telling her the news for the first time. "The Queen's Trea'." He looked at me. "Tending bar and learning the ropes of running a pub."

Jessica squeezed his arm and gazed at him with admiration. "We hope to run one together someday when we get a bit of dosh. I'm gonna start workin' at the base again to help with our bills."

"I'm so glad to hear it." And I was. "Wait 'til Jim hears the news. He will be very pleased for you both."

Walter and Kate strolled in together. They chuckled at some unheard joke and Kate put her head down in a gesture of shyness. I pointed to the two chairs across from mine.

Walter wore a horizontal-striped polo shirt and jeans. The shirt gave the illusion he had lost weight. Gone were the starched shirt and tie, pinstripe trousers, and suspenders. He carried an expensive iPad under his arm instead of the old-fashioned notebook that he normally held.

Well, I'll be. He's cut off his comb-over.

His face was relaxed as he pulled out a chair for Kate. She acknowledged the gesture with a bat of her eyelashes and a demure "Thank you," and slid under the table as she glanced my way, blushing with youthful color.

Walter's not wearing glasses either—must have gotten contacts. He looked ten years younger.

Turned out I was right; he wasn't a bad-looking man, and I was pleased my friend Kate was enjoying male company. Maybe my surprise garden party would be the time to announce some formal engagement or something between them. My imagination shot off and running with the speed of I'll Have Another, winner of the Kentucky Derby.

Jim rushed in, slightly out of breath. "Sorry I'm late, Dot. Had one more plant to tend to. Wanted to finish up."

The Crime Catchers were all in attendance.

Walter took everyone's drink orders and went to the bar to tell Roger while the rest of us settled in our seats. Bee-humming excitement buzzed on every side of the table. Wonder what kind of "honey" this group was going to make—especially between Kate and Walter. And what difference would we make in the life of a murderer in our village? Only time would tell.

I retrieved my notebook and began reviewing things, as I wanted to share before getting to the meat of the meeting and hearing everyone else's news. Besides, Lillie was chomping at the bit to share what she'd discovered.

The light coming through the window blinded me and I couldn't see the others. I shaded my eyes. "So glad everyone could make it."

Jim closed the window covering in order for me to see.

"Thanks, Jim. That's better. Where should I begin? Let me start by telling you what Jim and—"

Roger came to the table, pad in hand, and took our food orders and left.

"Now where was I?" I asked.

Kate helped me out. "I think you were going to tell us what you and Jim found out."

"Right." My memory could be as sharp as a new blade sometimes and as dull as a used razor at others. "First of all, most of you know the police discovered who was making those annoying phone calls. Looks like it was a prankster on a pay-as-you-go phone." Each nodded. "Secondly, Jim's officially a Crime Catcher since he's the one who discovered the criminal who broke our window."

Everyone turned in Jim's direction. He sipped his drink nonchalantly.

I smiled proudly at him. "Why don't you tell us?"

"How about I *show* everyone?" He tilted sideways, dug into his hip pocket, and brought out the white dimpled culprit—the golf ball.

"Where in the world did that come from?" Lillie placed her knitting needles into her bag on the floor near her feet, another row of stitches completed.

"Dotty's handbag." He lightly elbowed me and grinned. "Keep telling her she needs to get smaller ones."

"Jim's right ... about the golf ball, not about my bags." I tapped his arm in feigned annoyance. "I found three of the balls in our front garden and put them in my handbag as I was coming in and out of the house. In the madness of everything, I forgot about them. When I mentioned it to Jim this morning he went and dug one out of our sofa. We're pretty sure this is the deed doer." I took the ball from Jim and held it up. "With a little help from the boy around the corner from us." I handed it back to Jim and he put it back into his pocket.

Lillie clapped. "Isn't that great news, Jake?"

"Yes, dear."

"So that's two crimes solved, but neither of them had to do with the murders." Just as I said "murders" Roger showed up with the first round of food. Platters of fish, lasagna, and heaping salads took up the majority of the tabletop space. Fresh side dishes of steamed veggies were brought next. The broccoli was so green it looked as if it had just been plucked out of the field.

Lighthearted chatter replaced crime talk as condiments were passed and serviettes were laid across laps.

One thing I've learned is how to eat food with a fork and knife in hand. Americans tend to use a knife to cut their food and place the utensil down. British use the knife as an implement to help food sit on the back of the fork. Both are used at the same time. The knife pushes the food onto the fork and the fork goes straight into the mouth. Works rather efficiently, I might add.

Walter's and Kate's body language spoke volumes. Heads nearly touching, they seemed oblivious to anyone else at the table. Feeling as if I were intruding on an intimate moment, I lowered my eyes.

Once all the dishes were cleared from the table, I went back to the topic at hand: murder.

Chapter Forty-One

"Murder. That's what this meeting's all about."

The buzz of chattering stopped.

Everyone in attendance faced me with eagerness, particularly Lillie with her intensive Miss Marple stare. She sat on the edge of her chair. Pad and pencil, dug from her tapestry bag, were poised waiting to start.

"So much has happened since we last met. I'm thankful Jim's with us, and he's okay. Fortunately, it wasn't anything serious." As I touched his arm, he bowed his head as everyone clapped.

"I'm also proud to announce Fred's new job at the Queen's Treat." Fred beamed at my announcement. "We've got a lot to be grateful for, but we also have work that needs to be done. I want to hear what you've each found out, and what else we can do. So let's begin with Lillie."

I pencil-pointed in her direction.

She straightened, flipped open the pad of paper, and cleared her throat. "Well, you will all be interested to know . . ." Lillie paused for several seconds, wanting to be sure everyone was listening, "that…"

"What? Please tell us," Kate said.

"Amy Miser was an American."

Buzzing began again around the table.

I set my question slinger on fast mode. "How did you find out? Was she involved with Dan Swansey? Were they having an affair? Why was she here?"

Jim touched my hand. "Let her finish, Dot."

Roger came to take our dessert orders. The meeting would take an entire week with him interrupting every few minutes and Lillie deliberately stalling with her news.

Dessert ordered, everyone gaped at Lillie again, aching to know the details about Amy Miser.

"Please, Lillie, tell us what you found out," Jim said.

"Well, Jake and I were gone. Remember, Dotty? When Jim was in the hospital and I didn't call you straight away like I normally did?" She took a breath and looked at Jim. "By the way, I'm glad you're doing well."

Jim nodded. "Thanks. That's very kind. Please. Keep going."

"I have a friend—lives in Cornwall—who travels to the States quite often. Jake and I were visiting her and her husband. In fact, you might remember seeing them. We brought them to the Hare and Hound. They were visiting us at the time, but I didn't get a chance to introduce you to them. You and Jim were there that night, Dotty. Do you remember?"

I tapped into my computer brain retrieval cells. Nothing. "I'm not sure."

"Never mind. The first morning we were with them we were served the most delicious quiche with fresh fruit for breakfast."

Would she never get to the bottom of what she found out?

"As we were enjoying our relaxing meal our friend brought up the murders in East Lark. Out of the blue she says, 'I heard about Amy Miser.' So I told her we were trying to find out who killed Amy."

As much as I wanted to find out what Lillie knew, I had to interrupt. "What? Lillie, the Crime Catchers is supposed to be a *secret* group."

"Sorry. But this friend of mine—by the way, her name is Sue Morehead and her husband is John, and he's a lawyer—they're safe with our secret. Really, Dotty."

It's too late anyway, isn't it? Who knows how many other people you've told.

"Sue goes on to tell Jake and me, 'I know an Amy Miser.' Isn't that what she said, Jake?"

"Yes, dear."

"Well, we were both amazed. We asked Sue how she knew Amy. Apparently Sue is in California and she meets this Amy Miser at a party. Amy proceeds to tell Sue she's going to visit England. And of course Sue asks her where she'll be going. Amy says a small village in Suffolk called East Lark. So Sue tells her about us, maybe she could look us up when she comes on holiday. You know, that sort of thing."

Roger showed up carrying dishes stacked with enough sugar content to give us each a heart rush: sticky toffee puddings, ice cream with chocolate sauce, raspberry sponge, and coffees all around. Jim and I shared a sticky toffee pudding—me getting most of the share.

Dessert devoured, Lillie continued, "My friend Sue said Amy was coming here to meet a fellow she knew from the military. She met him at a place called the Defense Language Institute. Right, Jake?"

"Yes, dear."

"Didn't mean anything to me. Does it to you, Dotty?"

Lillie had not disappointed with her snooping skills, although this was more sheer luck than any real work. I said, "That's very interesting news. The Defense Language Institute is where Barbara met Dan. She told me the first time I met her at the village shop."

Lillie flipped her pad to the next page. "Turns out Amy was going to try and get a job so she could be with this man. Sue didn't mention anyone's name, but you're probably right. It must have been Dan."

My patience was waning. "What other person could it be? Especially since she's an American? Someone who knew a military person from the Defense Language Institute? There are too many coincidences."

Jim swallowed a large bite of pudding. "Good start, Lillie. It's more than we knew before. Right, Dot?"

He'd caught the tension in my voice.

"You're right, Jim. Thanks Lillie. I appreciate what you've found out. Is there anything else?"

Lillie wasn't finished. "There is one other thing."

Everyone said in unison, "What?"

"Apparently Amy Miser was involved with the law somehow. Not sure if she did something wrong or what. I told you Sue's husband was a lawyer. He knew Amy's name because of something he was working on. Of course he couldn't tell us too much—confidentiality and all that. Right, Walter?"

Walter lifted his eyes from his iPad. He was either taking notes or reading email. I couldn't tell. "You're right, Lillie. He most certainly could not say anything if it had to do with a court case or anything related to one."

Lillie sat back, closed her pad, and crossed her arms. "That about sums it up."

Thank goodness.

Chapter Forty-Two

"All of that is very useful, Lillie."

I jotted down some notes to review later. "At least we know now that Amy probably knew Dan, and most likely their murders are somehow related. Does everyone agree?"

Heads nodded in unison.

Once again Roger appeared like a genie out of a lamp to whisk away the emptied dessert dishes.

I looked at my watch. "Can you believe it's already one o'clock?"

Everyone looked at wristwatches.

"I've a meeting at two," Fred said. "Gotta be at the Queen's Treat by then."

"And I have ta go with him," Jessica added.

I carefully sipped my steaming coffee. "Let's move along then. Maybe we can try and keep our answers a bit shorter and quicker and not drag it out so much." I looked at Lillie, who was leaning down to her tapestry bag, pulling out her needles.

Jim side-kicked me.

"Ouch."

"Are you okay, Dotty?" Kate looked at me quizzically.

I picked up my cup and growled into the liquid. "I'm fine. Thanks. Let's keep going. Jake, were you able to find out anything about Arty? Where he comes from? What he did before coming to East Lark? Has he always been a postman?"

After each question Jake inhaled as if getting ready to answer, stopped, and waited until I fielded the next question. Seemed I was the one taking up too much time now.

Jake paused to be sure I'd finished. "Most of what I found out I learned from Jon at the shop. He knew Arty from his school days.

He told me he was a bit of a troublemaker but seemed to get his life in order the past few years when he began delivering mail."

Lillie spun toward him. "Jake Bakersfield, you never told me that."

Jake replied with firmness. "There are plenty of things you never let me get the chance to tell you or anyone else, Lillie."

An awkward silence filled the space around our little troupe.

Lillie dropped her needles onto her lap. "Gosh, Jake. I'm sorry. I do mean well." Her face held a mixture of astonishment and painful remorse.

Jake stared at her. His face twisted with anger, but he managed to keep his tone even. "Give me a chance to speak sometimes is all I'm trying to say."

"Yes, dear." A lone tear trickled down a long groove in her cheek.

Jake's chest filled as if it had been empty a very long time. He turned to the others. "Jon didn't know anything else. I did find out Arty was married, but now divorced. Guess it was a bitter separation. Morris filled me in on that small piece of information. Sorry I don't know more, but it's a start." He spoke confidently, like a man reborn.

"That's great, Jake." Jim knew how to get a conversation redirected after our many times of marital counseling with others. "What else is there, Dot?"

Jake's sharp response to Lillie had jolted my tempo. "Um, let's see." I glanced at Lillie out of the corner of my eye. Head held low, she twisted a hanky in her hands.

"Jessica? Did you and Fred learn anything about Barbara Swansey's job?"

Jessica looked at Fred. "We found out she works for some unit called OSI. Office of Investigation of some sort."

Fred nodded. "Some of the guys at the pub said she was working on a special project, but it's all they knew." He shrugged his shoulders. "Guess that's about it."

"That's plenty."

And they'd answered plenty of questions I had about Barbara's reluctance to talk about work. The OSI was the military's equivalent to the civilian FBI. Her undercover work added further intrigue to the whole situation.

"Did anyone say whether she or Dan were actually married, or maybe having problems in their marriage?"

Fred dug at a scar on the table's surface. "No one seemed to know. But that's no surprise. They never went to the pub together, as far as I know." He sat back. "Dan was such a ladies' man I'm sure his wife wouldn't wanna be seen with him. Wives know what their husbands are up to, whether the bloke realizes it or not. Right, Jessica?"

Jessica smiled at him, and used her index finger to twist a long strand of hair hanging alongside her face, and looked at me. "Sorry we couldn't find out more for you. Hope we can still be a part of this group?" She grabbed Fred's hand. "Since we didn' find out very much."

"Of course you're still a part of the Crime Catchers. We wouldn't dream of not having you with us. Would we?" I posed the question to everyone at the table.

Lillie's head rose. Her face had the post-crying sunburned look. For the first time she had lost her authoritative voice and spoke with the tone of a concerned mother. "Of course not. This group is important to all of us, and we need each other to figure out what's happened in our village. It's our home. And we are here to help Jim and Dotty. It's what neighbors and friends are for. Right?" She sniffled lightly.

Jim tapped my knee under the table. This time I didn't need his reminder that Lillie had a good heart. I felt extremely sorry for her, and for the fragile state her marriage was obviously in.

Jim said, "Besides, Jessica, all of this is very important."

"Lillie and Jim are right," I asserted. "I'm so pleased with what you found out. Every bit of information we have is another step toward helping the police with their investigation."

I jotted down in my growing notes what Fred and Jessica shared.

Last but not least, Walter needed to fill us in about the letter I had given him addressed to Dan Swansey.

I delayed a moment, as fear-filled goose bumps crept up my chest and neck. My voice wobbled. "I guess I'm a bit surprised I haven't gotten a call from the police about the letter, Walter. Did you give it to them? Did they want to know where you got it from?"

Walter laid his iPad on the table. As he was about to answer, I heard a familiar Irish brogue behind me. "Mrs. Weathervane, you are under arrest for the murder of Dan Swansey."

Chapter Forty-Three

Jim jumped up. His chair clattered then resettled back on its four legs.

He instinctively became a commander. Like riding a bicycle, it was something he never quite forgot. His arms hung alongside his puffed chest, and he stood at attention. "What are you talking about, Inspector O'Reilly? What's this all about?"

O'Reilly barked back, "That's *Chief* Inspector, Mr. Weathervane." He was probably hoping the one-upmanship of rank gave him more authority. "Your wife has withheld vital evidence in the murder of Dan Swansey."

Jim placed himself between O'Reilly and the back of my chair. "This is ridiculous."

O'Reilly tried to reach around Jim to touch my arm.

Jim shuffled in front of him. "Don't you dare touch my wife." His face was lodged within inches of O'Reilly's, and for a moment the other man must have lost his nerve as he hemmed and hawed—my view momentarily obstructed by Jim.

"By the way, how did you even know we were here?" It was Jim's turn to ask the questions. "And what makes you think my wife had anything to do with his murder?"

O'Reilly cleared his throat and reestablished his police bearing, speaking calmer but with firmness. "Mr. Weathervane, don't make this harder than it has to be."

"Tell me one good reason why you want to arrest my wife. She's hasn't done anything wrong."

Walter stood. "Dotty, I'm sorry. When I gave the letter to the police, I told them the truth, hoping they would understand and be sensible about it." He turned to O'Reilly. "You've got the wrong person here. Mrs. Weathervane is innocent and didn't have anything to do with these murders. I explained all of this at the station."

As O'Reilly started to respond, another voice came from the pub's opened door.

"Walter's right." Jonesy walked to the table.

"How dare you question my authority?" O'Reilly's ears would have spewed hot lava if they could have. "You don't have to worry about a promotion, PC. This will mean your job."

"Fine. Then I quit." Jonesy laid her badge on the table and stood with her hands on her hips. "You're . . . you're very difficult. That's all I'm going to say."

Gutsy, Jonesy. Always knew the girl had some spunk in her.

"I'm still arresting you, Mrs. Weathervane. For the murder of Dan Swansey."

O'Reilly must have wondered what hit him with the onslaught of verbal assault from the Crime Catchers.

I stood and patted the air with opened palms to calm everyone. "I was wrong to hold onto the letter." I turned to the chiseled-chin officer I'd thought was so attractive when I first met him. "I should have given the letter to you right away. It honestly was buried in my handbag. But I can tell you with all sincerity I had nothing to do with these murders, and I have a firm alibi if you're interested." My face was close to his and our eyes were locked.

"Mrs. Weathervane, where were you on the night Dan Swansey was killed? And who can verify your whereabouts?"

Jim clenched his teeth. "We answered the same question a million times when we were at the police station."

The chief inspector said to Jim, "Stay out of this." He turned to me. "I want to hear your answer firsthand."

"It's okay, Jim." I touched his cheek and answered O'Reilly. "I was with my husband. We were watching television."

He chuckled with fiendish glee. "Sorry, that's not much of an alibi. You and your husband could be in on this together."

"There's one other thing."

"What's that?" he growled.

"Dan Swansey was murdered at night, right?"

He shrugged his shoulders and sighed as if my question was stupid. "Of course."

"Well, there you go. I couldn't possibly have killed Dan Swansey or anyone else."

"And why not?"

"I can't go out at night. I'm afraid of the dark." And I was. Always had been. "In fact, I have a doctor's diagnosis to prove it. I've been told I have nyctophobia—fear of darkness, in case you don't know."

O'Reilly seemed to shrink.

The others stared at me.

Jim nodded and turned away.

Walter's judge-like voice brought a comfort to my ears. "O'Reilly, you owe this lady an apology. I told you when I brought the letter in that it was merely a mistake. Nothing more. Please reconsider your firing of PC Jones, too. She was upset at having a friend accused of a crime she didn't commit."

O'Reilly turned to Jonesy. "Meet me in my office in one hour. You've got an apology to write and some explaining to do. Don't forget your badge." He handed it to her.

"Yes, sir." Jonesy grabbed her badge and headed toward the door, but she stopped and said to me, "I knew you couldn't have anything to do with a murder."

"Go," O'Reilly spouted.

Jonesy dashed out of the pub.

The chief inspector used the voice of a drill instructor. "If I find out that you"—he pointed to me and everyone at the table—"or anyone here has anything to do with this murder or is withholding any more evidence, I will be back with a squad car and arrest the lot of you." He did an about-face and left with a little dignity still intact.

Chapter Forty-Four

Kate stood and we hugged.

Jessica and Lillie surrounded the two of us. It was a woman groupie thing that's not normally appealing to me. But I was ready to accept some W.E.T.—womanly estrogen tenderness.

Walter, Jake, and Fred stood awkwardly around Jim.

Walter said, "Sorry, Jim. I didn't mean for this to get out of control."

Jim shook Walter's hand. "You did what you had to do."

Fred gave a mini salute. "Jess and me have ta go. Le' us know when we're getting together again and what we can do ta help."

"Will do. Thanks, Fred."

Jessica and Fred began to leave. They stopped short of stepping out the door and looked back at me, both carrying worried looks across their faces as they turned and left the pub.

Jake came next. "Lillie and I have to go, too." He looked at Lillie and nodded first at her, then the door. "She and I have some things to talk about."

"Take it slow, Jake." Jim grabbed Jake's forearm.

"Will do. But it's been a long time coming."

Lillie clutched her bag to her chest and walked behind Jake out the door.

The only ones left were Kate and Walter.

Roger wiped off crumbs and splatters of water from the table with a cloth.

Walter talked quietly with Jim.

Kate whispered, "Dotty, I had no idea you had what-a-phobia. I thought we were good friends. Why didn't you ever tell me?"

I whispered back, "I didn't know I had it either."

Her eyes grew wide. "What are you talking about?"

"Well, it's true I don't care for the dark. It's also true I've been to the doctor and he told me phobia of the dark is called nyctophobia. Ergo I have nyctophobia. What do you think? Was I really telling a fib?"

"But Jim nodding his head made it appear that he agreed with you."

"I think he was trying not to laugh at O'Reilly's gullibility, actually."

Kate giggled.

"This goes to show, Kate, that we need to find out who committed these murders. O'Reilly is not going to be held off much longer if he thinks he can arrest me for Dan's death. We're going to have to figure out something. And soon."

Jim and I walked back home without saying a word.

Mr. Giles was running his tractor up and down the field. The seagulls swooped and dipped behind his trail.

A horse cantered past. The animal left a heap of steaming dung on the road and swished its tail as if to commend itself on a good job.

Jim took my hand.

Rapeseed fields were ripening, the unique and tangy smell beginning to fill the air as their golden tops swayed in the slight breeze.

Arriving home, Jim opened the front door for me and closed it behind us.

We walked into the kitchen and sat at the table, surrounded by the mess of an evil magician. I was glad to be home, although a murder charge had nearly separated Jim and me for a very long time from the life of leisure we had wanted to enjoy. And the real possibility of arrest was an option that still hung over our heads.

Chapter Forty-Five

Liquid sunshine.

That's what the optimist called it. The pessimist called it rain. It clattered on the French kitchen window with a vengeance. April showers bring May flowers. Here, spring showers killed any kind of flowers. Or at least battered them to death.

Jim stood at the window and sighed. "I'd hoped to work outside today."

"Nevermind." The two-made-into-one-word answer was one I picked up from Kate immediately after we became friends. It was a favorite response from any Brit in a situation where one had no control and nothing of real importance to say.

Jim turned to the kettle and began his Earl Grey routine.

I stared at my mug—the picture of the Queen when she was young and newly crowned smiled royally back at me.

Jim asked, "You okay, Dot?"

"Sure."

"Now I know something's wrong when *you* give *me* one-word answers." He sat at the table and placed his hands over mine wrapped around the coffee cup. "What's up?"

My head hung over the mug. "Wish I'd listened to you in the first place and never got involved."

"Dotty."

"If only we hadn't found the knife in the garden. If only I hadn't stopped and tugged the tie out of the bush and hadn't kept the letter in my purse. If only I minded my own business and stopped trying to help out. If only—"

"Dotty."

"If only I hadn't wanted to find out about Barbara and Dan or figure out who Amy Miser was." I looked up at Jim. "You always said you were attracted to my outgoing personality, but I don't know why." My head drooped again. "Gets me into trouble all the time. Then you have to come along and rescue me like a stray pup."

"Dotty."

"What?" Our eyes met.

"I didn't know we were having a party."

How'd he hear about the garden party?

I straightened. "What? How did you find out?"

"What?"

"About the party?"

"What party?"

"You just said you didn't know we were having a party."

"I meant a pity party. What did you mean?"

Oops.

"Nothing."

"What'd you think I meant?"

"Nothing."

Jim's questioning eyebrow rose to newer heights. He went to the boiling kettle and poured water for his tea. "She sure confuses me," I heard him mutter.

Whew. That was close.

But a good reminder to send out the invitations for the garden party I wanted to have in less than two weeks. The sofa would be delivered tomorrow. The window was finished. Hopefully the plants in the garden wouldn't wash down the street in a sea of rainwater and the actual day of the event would offer bright sunshine.

A party would be a great distractor from everything else, and I was happy to have something besides murder to keep me occupied.

I began humming Paul Simon's "I Am a Rock."

Jim smiled and winked.

+ + +

I stood by our French kitchen door window, and watched rain slide down the glass as tears slid down my face. I wept for Jake, for their family, and for the ways I had treated Lillie in the past. She was safely in the hospital. Her two younger sons, Benjamin and Nathan, accompanied her. The oldest son, Sam, was running errands. Jake was unsure of what to do, spinning in his own personal turmoil. There were many years of "yes, dear" that needed undoing and now was not the time.

Bliiiing.

"East Lark, 58 1808."

"Dotty." The voice was faint. "It's Lillie."

"Are you okay?"

"Jake wants a divorce."

"What? I'm sure it's only a temporary reaction. Jake didn't seem himself yesterday. Maybe Jim and I can talk to him?"

"He asked me not to call you." She whispered, "He's packing his things."

"We'll be right over."

"Thanks, Dotty."

+ + +

Jake opened the door, carrying an overstuffed tattered suitcase. The latch looked on the verge of popping open. "Lillie," he yelled back toward their kitchen. "This is another example of why I'm leaving. You never listen or do what I ask."

"Don't be mad, Jake." Jim's pastor voice was like a hypnotist speaking to a client. The client listens then obeys what he is told to do. "Please put your bag down and let's talk." Jake set the bag down.

I went into the kitchen. Several stainless steel pots were sitting on the black Aga stove. Steam rose from the largest and the smell of cooking cabbage permeated the room. Not the most pleasant of odors in my estimation.

Lillie paced her large farmhouse kitchen like a trapped animal, twisting a hanky in her hand and crying. She was moving quickly toward a nervous breakdown and into a world of her own making.

I recognized the symptoms, as she repeated, "What am I going to do? What am I going to do?"

"Lillie? Jim is talking with Jake right now. What happened?"

She spoke more to herself than me. "I'm not sure. We came home from the meeting yesterday. Jake didn't say anything. This morning he had his bags opened at the foot of the bed."

"Lillie."

She stopped. "What? Dotty? When did you get here?"

"Listen to me very carefully, Lillie." I held her arms, trying to help her concentrate.

She nodded.

"Everything will be okay, even if Jake decides to go away for a few days. Everything will be okay. Do you understand?"

She pushed away and continued pacing.

Jake and Jim entered the kitchen. Jake looked at us with questioning eyes. "I've never seen her like this before." He walked over and touched Lillie's shoulder. She shrugged his hand off and kept moving around the kitchen.

Jim said, "Jake, Lillie might need some medical help. And you may not want to hear this, but she needs you more than ever. You need to call Mr. Carlton and have him or one of the other doctors come over."

Jake left the room, and we heard him speaking on the phone to the doctor's office.

"Will she be okay?" I looked at Jim.

"She's going to need plenty of rest and care. We must let their sons know that their mother isn't well and they'll need to help their dad in any way they can."

"Okay. I'll tell them once I'm sure Lillie's settled a little."

"Let me see what Jake found out." Jim left the kitchen.

"Sometimes being the 'couples' couple' is not an easy task," I said to no one in particular as Lillie paced and twisted her hanky.

+ + +

I stood by our French kitchen window, and watched rain slide down the glass as tears slid down my face. I wept for Jake, for their family, and for the ways I had treated Lillie in the past. She was safely in the hospital. Her two younger sons, Benjamin and Nathan, accompanied her. The oldest son, Sam, was running errands. Jake was unsure of what to do, spinning in his own personal turmoil. There were many years of "yes, dear" that needed undoing and now was not the time.

Bliiiing.

"East Lark, 58 1808."

"Dotty." Kate's Julie Andrews voice soothed me. "I just heard about Lillie. Their son Sam was at the shop and he told me what happened. Is there anything I can do for them?"

"Thanks, Kate. Jim is with Jake. I thought I'd bring them a meal tomorrow. If you want to fix something for this evening, then they should have enough home cooking to last a few days. I can't imagine the four men in the house are thinking about food right now, but they will when the time comes to eat. And I can't imagine Lillie letting any of them in the kitchen to cook, so they probably don't know how."

"I'll bring something over today. If you can think of anything else just let me know."

"Thanks. I know the family will appreciate it."

We hung up.

There's something positive to be said about going to a tropical island, away from the anxiety and fears of life, to retire.

A place where there was no one or nothing but fat coconuts hanging from palm trees, warm breezes blowing over cool ocean waves, and a good book.

But then again, I wouldn't have friends like Kate, Vivian, and yes, even Lillie. The sacrifice of a perfect, idyllic setting was worth the investment of knowing some wonderful people who cared for me and for one another.

Chapter Forty-Six

BBC played softly in the background as we finished our quiet breakfast. Jim left the newspaper untouched.

I prepared a meal for the Bakersfields and set off to drop the lasagna casserole, salad, and breadsticks at the farm.

Sam, the oldest, answered the door and took my offerings. "Ta. Dad's out in the field caring for the crops. Benjamin and Nathan are helping him."

"How's your mom? Still in the hospital?"

"Yes, but they think she might be home within a week."

"I'm glad to hear it." And I was.

And it was a good sign that Jake hadn't left.

I drove home without hitting curbs or killing fowls.

Back in my kitchen I flitted from stacks of *Break* to stacks of papers—newspapers and personal types that needed filing.

Finally, I went to the window and watched Jim kneeling in the dirt.

He used the garden as a coping mechanism. It was a place for him to go where his thoughts could wander, perhaps consider his time with Jake after Lillie was hospitalized and the long chats they'd had.

Jim's muscles moved under his T-shirt as he dug. The man might be aging, but his muscles stayed toned working alongside Mother Nature and caring for his garden. Perhaps Mother Nature and I should spend some time together. I could use some muscle toning myself.

I filled out invitations for the upcoming surprise garden party for Jim, and addressed one to the Bakersfields. I hoped Lillie would be able to attend and Jake would come with her.

+ + +

I took a quick trip to the village shop for stamps and to mail the invites.

The chatter and gossip at the shop did not cheer me up or tempt me to stay and listen. Nothing seemed relevant. Talk was merely about the latest banger race coming to the track. Who cared?

When I arrived home, a Harvey's Furniture truck was parked in front of the house; the sofa, covered in what looked like a horse blanket, was being lugged out the van's cavernous back door.

The deliverymen had difficulty getting the couch through the front door. They took off the doweled feet, twisted it sideways, and barely managed to squeeze it in without damaging the doorframe.

We signed off on the delivery, ate lunch, and Jim headed back to the garden.

After grabbing a pad of paper and stack of recipe clippings from *Break,* I headed to the living room. Normally the kitchen table served as my primary desk, but I wanted to enjoy our new sofa and a window that no longer whistled. At least a few things were getting back to normal.

I finished with the recipes and a list of ingredients, and began a checklist for the next Crime Catchers get-together.

In many ways it seemed ages ago we'd had our last meeting—with Lillie's hospitalization and everything that had happened since then.

I scribbled:

First: When and where to meet next? Kate's house?

Second: What other details did we need to find out? There were so many questions left unanswered.

I tucked the two lists into the pad of paper and closed my eyes.

The soft brown leather cushion sank with the softness of Charmin. The smell of new leather drifted to my nostrils and the silence was relaxing. *Ahh.*

A familiar smell tickled my nose.

I opened one eye.

Jim stood over me holding a cup of coffee. "You okay?"

"Yep, must have dozed off. Just making sure we like our new purchase." I patted the arms and went into the kitchen, mug in hand, following Jim.

Reruns of *Midsomer Murders* ended our day and made me think of Lillie and how much she loved the show. She always wanted to visit the towns and villages where the program was filmed, and I hoped she would one day get her wish. Maybe she and Jake could do the trip together someday, for fun—something sorely lacking in their marriage.

With the show over our bed beckoned, and so did sleep.

Chapter Forty-Seven

The French doors were wide open; songs of finches, sparrows, and blackbirds filtered into the kitchen and sun spilled onto the floor.

I chewed the pencil while jotting notes.

Lillie and Jake's friends: John (lawyer) and Sue Morehead from Cornwall.

Sue Morehead meets American Amy Miser at a party in California.

Amy Miser tells Sue Morehead she's coming to East Lark.

She comes to England to meet up with a man—no name. Was killed. Why?

Jim was buried behind the news. He lowered the corner and peered around the paper.

"What?" I asked.

"Could you please stop gnawing? It makes it difficult to concentrate." Up the corner went.

"Fine."

Amy Miser knew a guy from Defense Language Institute, and was involved with the law.

The pencil went toward my mouth. I stopped it midway.

Down the newspaper went. "What are you doing, anyway?"

"Rewriting my notes from the meeting. It helps me think."

Up the paper went.

Jake found out Arty Smith was a troublemaker in school.

Arty straightened out after getting the postal job.

Difficult divorce.

I left the spiral-bound notepad on the table, turned on the hot tap, and turned up the radio. Classical music soothed the savage beast and gave my mind a rest.

Cups and dishes clinked as I placed them in the sink. I wrapped an apron around my waist and snapped on rubber gloves.

Jim folded his paper, grabbed his tools, and opened the back door. Walter practically fell into the house, his hand still formed into a knuckle ready to rap.

His cherry nose was Rudolph reindeer red as he caught himself just before splatting on the hardwood floor. "Oh, dear. I'm so sorry."

Jim set down his tools. "Are you all right? What a pleasant surprise. Come in." He directed Walter to a chair. "Would you like something to drink? A cup of tea or coffee?"

Walter was casually dressed. Jeans, country-western-type shirt, and cowboy boots. Each time I saw him, his style had changed further away from the starched-shirt, tie-wearing magistrate we'd first met.

Hmm. Wonder what he'll be wearing next time I see him. A toga?

I pulled my cleaning gloves off and restarted the kettle.

"Actually I came to see you, Dotty."

I felt my blood rush from my face. My knees nearly buckled. "Me?" I swallowed hard. "Does this have to do with the police and the letter? Are they coming for me? Do I need to go and pack? What's going on?"

Jim placed his arm around my shoulder. "Dotty, give the man a chance to speak."

Walter stood. "Oh, dear. It's nothing like that. I'm so sorry I frightened you. Maybe I shouldn't have come."

"Please sit, Walter, and tell us what this is all about." Jim put a cup of tea in front of him. "You're welcome to visit any time, but you can imagine we are a bit jittery after the incident at the pub with O'Reilly."

Walter sat. "I most certainly understand."

I slid into the chair across from him. "What is it? What can I do for you?"

He cleared his throat. "It's about Kate."

"What about her?" I tried not to sing "hallelujah" and clap with glee.

"Well, I'm not sure how to say this."

"Go ahead, man, tell us what's on your mind," Jim said.

Redness reappeared on Walter's nose and spread across his cheeks. He spoke quickly, as if he didn't want to chicken out at the last minute. "I wondered if you could tell me if she has a man in her life? I mean is she dating anyone? Is there anyone of interest I should know about? I've been alone for a very long time and . . ."

"Well, I'll be." Jim sat back and smiled. "Kate, huh?"

Walter slowed. "Guess what I'm trying to ask is—"

"Yes?" I rushed him.

"Do you think I have a chance with her?"

Suddenly he looked to be about twelve to me, with the childish uncertainty of a boy who wanted to be accepted and loved.

"Why don't you ask her out?" I gently assured him. "I believe you'll be happy to hear what she has to say."

"Really?" The mature man was back and with him a level of certainty. "All right then. I'll do it. Thanks. Both of you."

As quickly as he had come, he was gone. The tea left untouched.

Jim and I looked at each other, smiled knowingly, and went back to our tasks at hand: me to the sink, him to sinking in the earth with his plants.

Chapter Forty-Eight

I checked off my to-do list: dishes done, recycling bags removed, and the kitchen sparkled.

Once again I found myself at the table chewing on a pencil.

Barbara works for OSI.

Never went out with Dan—to the pub at least. Bad marriage? Any marriage?

I slipped my shoes off. The bunion throbbed with drum-beating rhythm.

There were several missing pieces to the murder puzzle. I had to figure out what questions to ask in order to get the answers we needed.

From what Lillie found out from her friend Sue Morehead, Dan and Amy probably knew each other from the Defense Language Institute. But did Barbara learn that Amy was having an affair with Dan and killed them?

I wrote frantically before my ideas vaporized. What about Arty? He was divorced. Who was his ex-wife? Could it be Amy? He and Dan were overheard fighting but no one knew what the fight was about. I filled the pad of paper with haphazard guesses.

I reluctantly put aside my list of questions and moved ahead with my day.

First, I rang Kate and invited her over for a cuppa to ask her advice about my party invitees and, of course, ask her about Walter.

+ + +

The back door creaked open. Jim walked into the kitchen.

"Shhh, Kate. It's Jim," I warned her.

Jim said, "Dotty? What are you and Kate doing?"

I slapped the pad of paper with the garden party guest list closed. "Um. Talking."

"I can see that." He shook his head, did an about-face, and went back outside.

"That was close." Kate giggled.

"I've been trying to put this thing together for weeks and something always seems to come up."

Kate's dimple deepened. "Jim will appreciate all the hard work you've done."

"I hope so. I mailed the invitations yesterday and realized I might have forgotten someone. I don't want to leave anyone out or hurt anyone's feelings. But with your help, it looks like I invited everyone I should." I tore the paper with the names out of the notepad and folded it. "Now . . ."

"What?"

"Have you heard from Walter recently?"

"No. I haven't seen him since the meeting at the pub." Kate got up and restarted the kettle. "Why do you ask?"

"It's strange, that's all."

Kate poured hot water into my cup. "What's strange?"

"Walter stopped by—"

"Dotty." The word cracked like the snap of a dried branch. Jim stood on the threshold, hands on hips. "Do you think you need to share what you were about to say?"

"What? I wasn't doing anything wrong." I batted my eyes at him in hopes of deflecting a commander's "call to attention."

"You know precisely what I'm talking about." He stepped to the sink with a watering can. "I need to get some warm water."

"What are you two talking about?" Kate finger-brushed her bangs along her forehead. "Seems like I missed something."

"It's nothing. By the way, can we have our next Crime Catchers meeting at your place? Say a week from today?"

She looked first at Jim then me. "Certainly." She seemed to be waiting to see if we were going to say anything else and shrugged.

"I suppose I better go. It is lunchtime and I need to take care of the horses. By the way, Dotty, the next horse competition will be in a couple of weeks. It's being held in Newmarket. I'll let you know the date if you are interested."

"Of course I'm interested." I patted my own hair and a large curl flipped into my face. Another trip to Fiona's would have to happen before then. "I always enjoy coming."

"Maybe I can get you on one of my horses sometime?"

"Not on your life or the life of your poor animal. If I have trouble driving a car I can't imagine what I'd do on the back of a thousand pounds of horsepower."

Kate giggled. "I will be sure to give you the details about the competition. And we can chat more about having the Crime Catchers meeting at my place, too."

"Thanks for coming by, Kate."

"You're sure you have nothing else you want to tell me? About Walter?" She looked at me, then Jim.

We shook our heads no.

Jim's fists were resting on his hips. The water ran in the sink. "That was very close, Dotty Weathervane."

"What? Why couldn't I tell her about Walter stopping by?"

Jim shut off the tap. "What if Walter lost courage and decided not to ask her out? Don't you think she'd be even more disappointed if she was interested?"

"Didn't think about that."

"There are times, Dotty . . ." Jim dropped the subject.

He turned to the filled watering can and lugged it outside.

I lifted myself out of the chair. "Guess I'll just have to wait and see what happens between her and Walter. There's nothing I can do about it now."

Chapter Forty-Nine

Mail pushed through the front door's letter slot needed to be retrieved and with it another bout of exercise.

Flyers and leaflets from Pizza Hut, Suzie's Sushi, and Co-Op Supermarket were piled inside the entranceway, along with personal pieces of mail.

Our post was delivered late in the day, right when I was ready to put aside any tasks and take it easy. It was my time to read or write a few lines for the romance novel I still mulled over writing. Walter and Kate would be the basis of my story. Magistrate meets beautiful lady in dressage amidst a murder investigation. How romantic was that?

Instead, I flipped through the mail and piled it into two stacks on the table: recycling and bills.

As I headed to the recycling bag with a stack of papers, a single sheet fell from the pile and landed on the floor. I stooped and picked it up.

A piece of lined pink paper with rose petals on opposite corners had chicken-scratch writing:

Dotty, please meet me at the village hall at 6:00. Vivian.

"That's strange." I looked at my watch. 5:30.

There's plenty of time to get there.

I stepped out the open French kitchen doors. "Jim?"

He stood in the center of the garden, his back to the house, swinging back and forth from the waist to scan his garden canvas of flowers. A splash of color somewhere along the border would last several months. Potted plants stood by the summerhouse and offered a welcoming sight for a place to rest and relax. Without me even realizing it, my little idyllic island had been in the back garden all along.

"Jim? Everything looks so lovely." Silence.

"I'm heading to the hall. Vivian wants me to meet her there at six o'clock. I guess they must be deciding what to do for the upcoming opening. Maybe the Women's Institute is taking care of decorations or something."

Jim continued to scan his artistic masterpiece and backhandedly waved.

Back inside, I turned on the oven, picked up a few things off the table, and set the dishes out for dinner. Peppers from Peter's veggie stand filled with rice, feta cheese, and onions sat ready to be cooked.

A quick look in the front hall mirror reinforced the opinion Fiona had to do something once again with my mop of unruly hair.

I stepped out the front door. The young rider last seen wearing a fluorescent pink Jane Fonda's sixties outfit rode in front of the house. I waited for her to pass. Her posture was perfect. She tapped her riding hat, now a polished black helmet, as thanks.

As the horse clopped by I watched marshmallow clouds morph into various shapes, the wind moving quickly through the sky. Blue, bordering on purple, played peek-a-boo between the moving clouds.

Daylight flicked off the solar panels, and the sky's reflection was captured in the glass. Checking the front door of the hall and finding it locked, I circled the building.

The bolt on the back door had been replaced after the recent break-in, but the lock was open and the door ajar.

I stepped into the semi-dark room. "Vivian? Hello."

The hanging bare bulbs were long gone. Now half-domed fixtures lined the length of each wall as far as I could see. Currently the only lighting came from two wall-lamps behind the raised stage area where Walter had pounded his gavel with such relish during the Neighborhood Watch meeting. The rest of the room was gradually darker, the far end of the long room in total blackness.

I blinked, adjusting my eyes to the darkness.

"Vivian?"

I eased my way along.

Rattle. Rattle. Crash.

"Vivian? Is that you?"

A chill ran up my back.

I turned to leave. The hinges creaked and the door slammed shut.

Chapter Fifty

"Vivian?" The word stuck in my windpipe.

A pinpoint of light twinkled by the closed door.

"Dotty?"

A familiar shape emerged.

"Barbara?" *Gulp*.

She held a small flashlight in her hand, attached to a large set of keys.

"I ... I ... I'm looking for Vivian." I backed away as she approached. "What are you doing here?"

Barbara stepped closer. Her shiny patent leather heels clicked on the hardwood floor. The light illuminated her figure.

She wore a more formal uniform. "What are you talking about?"

"I was supposed to meet Vivian." I swallowed. Fear tasted like chicken. Chicken sitting in a compost heap for a week. Not that I ever tried it but nothing else could taste this bad. "I asked you, what . . . what are you doing here?"

Barbara directed the light into my eyes. I was blinded to her expression as she moved closer.

"Dotty, you asked me to come."

"No, I didn't. Why are you saying that?" I blocked the light with an outstretched hand. For such a small LED it had a powerful beam.

She dropped the flashlight to waist level. "I had a note in my mailbox to meet you here at six o'clock."

I went into the small light's ray and stepped closer. "I didn't send any note asking you to come. But I got a note, too. To meet Vivian here."

Her lopsided grin was one of annoyance and amusement. "This is somebody's idea of a bad joke, I guess."

"Whew." I exhaled. "I was a bit scared there for a minute."

"Nothing to be afraid of. Let's go. I have a meeting I'm already late for."

I gave a nervous chuckle. "And I'm late fixing Jim's dinner. He'll be wondering where his food is."

"Can't have that now, can we?" An unseen person from the back of the room with a high-pitched, singsong voice spoke. "In fact, you might never fix him another dinner again."

"Who are you?" Barbara and I asked at the same time.

"Turn the light off, Captain Swansey," the voice in the dark ordered, "and you won't be hurt."

I whimpered. "You better do it."

Barbara clicked off the light.

"Now slide it across the floor."

She did as she was told. The keys rattled as she threw them, sounding like the chains worn by Marley frightening Scrooge in *A Christmas Carol*.

The voice dictated, "Now turn around and face the other way."

We turned. I grabbed Barbara's hand. She squeezed and whispered, "It will be okay, Dotty, as long as we stay calm and do as we're told."

"Be quiet. I mean it," the high-pitched voice ordered.

The next thing I knew a black cape was draped over my head. The lights on the platform a mere blur.

I screamed, "I can't stand the dark!" I grabbed Barbara's hand.

"Shut up," the person yelled in my ear. "Or I'll stuff a gag in your big mouth. You two couldn't mind your own business, could you?"

"What are you talking about?" I squealed. "We don't even spend much time together. What business are we involved in?"

Hands pushed me down on a chair, and Barbara's fingers released from mine. I sensed her beside me, but I guessed her hands and feet were tied with ropes like mine were.

"I've got to figure out how to get rid of the two of you without anyone suspecting foul play." The shadowed, mysterious person moved back and forth, blocking the dim light each time.

The shadow stopped. "Can't have two more murders added to the other two, can we? This needs to be an accident."

I opened my eyes as wide as I could, trying to see through the black hood. All I managed to do was hurt my eyes and give myself a headache.

The person moved two or three steps away. "If a fire started from an electric shortage it would look natural." The rubbing of hands could be heard. "Too bad I might have to damage this building after all the hard work they've put in fixing it." *Chuckle.*

I shuffled in my chair.

Our abductor said, "Sit still. I have to go and get some things. I'll be back shortly. Don't you two go anywhere." *Chuckle.*

I squeaked, "The ropes are tight on my hands. Can you loosen them before you go?"

"Mine too," Barbara added, shuffling in her chair.

The person yapped, "Be quiet. Both of you. Do you think I'm stupid? In a little while you aren't going to have to worry about your hands hurting."

I whimpered as the back door opened and closed.

It was quieter than the Stonehenge burial site at high noon.

Barbara whispered, "Dotty? You okay?"

"Yes. You? Who was that? Did you recognize the voice? Wasn't it odd? A man with a woman's pitch, don't you think?" My questioning gun was set on rapid fire. I could hear Jim in my mind saying, "Dotty, slow down." I took a deep breath. "Sorry, Barbara.

I always ask a multitude of questions when I'm nervous, scared, happy. Any time actually."

Her chair shuffled. "It's okay. I know you're scared. I am, too. But we'll get out of this mess. Somehow. We're New Yorkers, right?"

"You're right." I released a sigh of relief knowing Barbara was with me. "Does anyone know you're here, so they'll be coming looking for you?"

"No. I was heading to a meeting, so they'll wonder where I am though. How about Jim? Does he know you came to the hall?"

"I told him, but I don't think he heard me."

I wasn't sure whether to be upset with Jim or worried for him when he realized I was gone. When he was taken to the hospital I was beside myself with anxiety. I knew he would be dealing with the same feelings about me—maybe more. How many times had he told me, "I worry about you, Dot. That's all." If only he knew how much he should be worrying about me right now, he'd have plenty to keep him busy.

I wasn't as convinced as Barbara that we would get out of this situation. After all, who would come to the village hall this time of day? The place was dark, the door probably locked, and we were potentially facing the licking flames of death. What a way to go. I always imagined a much more dramatic ending for my life than being a shish kebab in a newly renovated coffin called a village hall.

Come to think of it, this would be a pretty dramatic ending after all. I shivered.

Chapter Fifty-One

The hall creaked.

Creepy-crawling shivers made hairs on the back of my neck tingle. "Did you hear that?"

"Yes," Barbara whispered.

"Do you think anyone else is in here?"

"I think we'd know by now if there was, don't you?"

My shoulders relaxed slightly. "I'm sure you're right. I hate the dark, that's all."

"Does it help to talk?"

I tried to speak evenly, but my voice trembled. "Yes. And I want to say, I'm so sorry."

She sounded surprised. "For what?"

"For thinking badly of you. I thought maybe you had something to do with Dan's death. You frightened me when you first came in the hall. I thought you were going to hurt me too."

"Dotty, I totally understand."

"You do?"

"Of course. And I hope you believe me when I tell you that I had nothing to do with any of this. Although Dan's and my marriage was certainly a sham from the start."

Barbara's self-assured tone turned acidic. "He was so charming when we first met. I was swept off my feet, believed his lies. Others tried to warn me of his womanizing, but I thought they were jealous that he wanted to marry me."

"I'm so sorry for all of this."

"I had hoped things would get better once we got here and had a chance to spend some time together. But they didn't."

"What happened?"

"Our marriage only got progressively worse. When I found out what he was involved with I had divorce papers drawn up. He got them the day he was killed."

"That's awful. For both of you."

A long pause made me wonder if Barbara was reconsidering her decision.

"But why'd you imagine I had anything to do with these murders, Dotty?"

"Do you want the truth?"

"Of course."

"I assumed Dan and Amy were having an affair, and you acted out of jealousy. What other conclusion could there be?"

"How did you know Amy and Dan knew each other?"

"It's a long story."

Barbara's deep sigh echoed through the hall. "Actually, you've got it all wrong."

"I do?"

"You might want to know I'm an OSI agent. That's why I was asking you all those questions about folks in the village. I'd been doing some investigating to find out how much you knew."

"I know all that."

"You do?" She clicked her tongue. "Why am I not surprised?"

I pulled on my hand ropes, my wrists getting raw from the rub. "We were trying to find out anything we could, so the police wouldn't think Jim and I killed Dan and Amy. O'Reilly seemed to be pursuing us like a hound dog."

Barbara tugging on her ropes shadowed through my hood. "You're right about Amy coming here."

"So you knew it was Dan she came to see?"

"Yes."

I stopped tugging to catch my breath. "Didn't it upset you? Even if your marriage was bad? I know I'd hate Amy if I were you."

"She wasn't coming here as Dan's lover. Even if she was, I had gotten use to Dan's philandering and stopped loving him a long time ago. Her coming was part of the plan."

"What plan?"

The smell of body odor from fear and struggling was beginning to fill my immediate space.

"Amy was an OSI agent too. In fact, she was a very good friend of mine. She was here undercover looking into some of Dan's dealings."

"What dealings?"

She paused. "Guess it doesn't matter if I tell you. We're either going to get out of this, in which case we'll have our killer, or we won't. Dan had connections."

"What kind?"

"With the British mafia."

"Mafia? I thought they were only in New York."

"Ever hear of Cocky Warren? The media calls him Britain's most successful gangster. Actually he's a Ken doll compared to others who've infiltrated the shores of the UK in recent years, guys from America, Russia, and other places. When Dan was still active duty, he had several interactions with some professional gangsters, then began his own business interactions with these goons before he resigned his commission."

"What was Amy going to do?"

"She was a honey trap for him. She was absolutely beautiful. Dan was attracted to her like hummingbirds to sugar." Hostility entered her voice whenever she said Dan's name. "We were trying to catch him in the act of gambling, drugs. The racecourse was a good cover-up for him. He used it as a means to track monies coming into and out of the area. We were getting close to having enough evidence to convict him and suddenly he was killed. Then Amy." She sniffled.

"I'm so sorry about your friend."

"Shhh." Barbara's voice trembled. "Did you hear that?"

If blood froze, mine would have resembled a cherry Popsicle. "Was that the door?"

We were like two coyotes trapped in a snare waiting for the hunter to return.

+ + +

"Miss me?" Our high-pitched-voiced captor was back.

Barbara and I shuffled and squealed.

"Don't worry, ladies. This won't take long."

A shadowed figure neared.

I leaned back. My chair teetered and began tilting. I screamed, and hands grabbed my arms just before the chair collapsed.

"Sit still, you fool," the singsong voice said.

"Dotty? Are you okay?" Barbara hollered.

"I'm fine."

The shadow moved from view. "Now where was I?"

Rustling sounds of paper and the smell of phosphorous.

"What're you doing?" I screamed.

Without warning the door opened and closed, and light briefly entered the room. A rush of cold air slapped my legs.

Someone approached. Two shadows were now in view.

"What in the world are you doing?"

This voice I recognized.

I tried to shout but raspy sounds escaped instead. "Walter? Is that you? Thank goodness. You've got to stop this imbecile from burning us alive."

Chapter Fifty-Two

"Walter! We're so glad you're here. Untie us. Please," Barbara said. "Tell whoever this is that we aren't involved with these murders."

"I'm afraid I can't do that," Walter said.

"What? What do you mean?" I gasped.

"I'm sorry it's come to this, Mrs. Weathervane. Captain Swansey." Walter's voice was crisp. "I was hoping to spare you. In fact, I've grown quite fond of you and Jim, *Dotty*."

I thrashed and almost tipped my chair again. "What are you talking about? Please. Let Barbara and me go. What's this all about anyway?"

"You fool." Walter spoke to the other person. "Why couldn't you wait like I told you to?"

The high-pitched person whined with the hissy fit of a two-year-old. "They were getting too close. You heard them talking at the pub. They were getting suspicious."

"They were nowhere near knowing *I* was involved. In fact, they were starting to trust me, felt sorry for me. Thought I was a lonely widower." Walter chuckled. "And I was this close to asking Kate out to dinner. Then you ring me and tell me you've lured them here. You moron."

A slap. The high-pitched voice sniveled.

I started crying.

"You've got it all wrong, Walter Reed," Barbara growled. "We were closing in on you and you knew it. It was only a matter of time before we had you."

Tears of fear turned to waves of anger. "Not me. I didn't suspect a thing. How dare you take advantage of Jim and me? And Kate?"

Walter placed his hands on my knees and spoke into the hood, inches from my face. If I could, I would've bitten his nose off. "You were so naïve. It was easy."

His aftershave made my already weak stomach worse.

He snickered. "I saw you looking at me at the pub when I was hanging over that pint, acting pathetically drunk. I should've won an Oscar. I heard every word you and Jim said."

"You creep."

"When you invited me to be a part of The Crime Catchers, gave me the letter with Dan's name, well, you made it easy."

I swung my feet up and smashed his shins.

"Yeow." He lifted his hands off.

"That's for making me think you're a nice guy."

He stepped away.

The other assailant was getting nervous, stomping his feet and flailing his arms. "You heard her. She said they were getting close."

Another slap. "They're both lying, you idiot."

"Stop hitting me. Look, man, I did everything you told me. I put the knife in Weathervane's hedge, the other things under the bush. Wrote the fake letter with Dan Swansey's name on it. You had everything perfectly laid out to put suspicion on them."

"Why would you want to do this?" I asked. "Have we ever done anything to make you want to hurt us, Walter?"

He leaned back into my face again. "You were always so *nice*, Dotty."

The singsong voice chimed in. "You and Jim were the perfect setup. Who wouldn't suspect *Americans* living here once news got out the mafia had dealings in this village?"

"But why Barbara?" I asked.

"She was always asking questions, always wanting to know about folks in the village. Asked me a couple of times about Walter but I shrugged her off." The high-pitched sound was beginning to grate on my nerves.

Walter snarled. "Be quiet. You imbecile. Don't say anything else."

"It doesn't matter. We know it all anyway. Don't we, Dotty?" Barbara egged them on.

"Um, of course we do. I was lying earlier when I said I didn't know anything. The Crime Catchers had meetings without you, Walter. We were trying to trap you in—"

The stranger interrupted, "What difference does it make? You'll both be gone soon, and no one will be the wiser."

"You're so wrong. There're plenty of people who know what's going on." Barbara continued to push.

I whispered, "Are you sure this is a good idea?" Beads of sweat rolled down my armpits and back.

Walter pulled the hoods off our heads. "What are you two talking about?" His khaki pants and beige short-sleeve shirt were neatly ironed. But the look on his face was not of a young boy wanting love and acceptance. Instead, it was old and haggard, his mouth twisted in surly disfigurement.

Barbara raised her voice defiantly. "I was on my way to meet with Chief Inspector O'Reilly and officials with MI5. The OSI, police, and MI5 were in a joint operation. We were getting together to prepare a warrant for your arrest, Walter."

"You're making this all up."

"We knew you were originally a part of Cocky Warren's gang and then split from him to start your own syndicate with Dan. Just didn't have enough evidence to convict you on drug running and money laundering. Then we got a break. Dan spilled things to Amy about everything: the money, drugs, and the racecourse. He was so taken by her; he couldn't keep his mouth shut. Somehow you found out Dan was blabbing to Amy, so you had to get rid of them both." She shuffled in her seat. "It was only a matter of time to get enough evidence to tie you to the murders. You were so cocky yourself using a tie, weren't you? Like you were taunting us. We knew it was your trademark."

"I get the tie, Barbara. Walter always wore them, until recently. But why the stockings?"

She practically spit in Walter's face. "The stockings he used were Amy's favorite, but only someone close to her would know that. She loved anything retro, and nylons were one of those fetishes she had—always bought French Cervin for special occasions. Dan must have mentioned it before Walter killed him. The tie was Walter's trademark. The stockings were hers."

The other man came from behind to face us. If it had been my long deceased mother-in-law, I wouldn't have been nearly as surprised as I was with our original assailant.

Chapter Fifty-Three

"You had no idea he was involved, did you?" Walter prodded, pointing to none other than Roger Lacey, owner of the Hare and Hound.

"You always were dying to eat at the pub, weren't you, Mrs. Weathervane?" Roger squealed with delight.

"You?"

Roger never spoke to me although I'd often tried to talk to him. I figured he wasn't interested or didn't have the wherewithal to chat with women. Guess he was keeping his distinctive voice hidden.

"See, she had no idea you were involved, Roger. We could have gotten away with all of this if you'd just been patient." Walter slapped Roger again.

"Stop doing that," Roger squalled.

"What are you going to do about it? You big girl's blouse," Walter teased.

"If you hit me again I'm going to . . ."

The two men began a face-off, their noses nearly touching.

Walter's fists sat on his hips. "What are you going to do? Whip me with a soggy chip? You smell like a load of fish and chips." His stomach jiggled in time with his fiendish laugh.

Roger reached to hit him.

I shouted, "Calm down, gentlemen."

Roger dropped his hand and looked at us with sinister intent. His toupee-looking hair hung this way and that. His long arms and short legs made him look like a monkey.

"She's right," Walter said. "We need to get rid of these two now that you've brought them here. Let's burn this place down and get out while we can. We're going to need to leave East Lark, head to London, and spend some time under a rock somewhere. We'll meet up again in a few months."

"You're certainly going to spend time under a rock, but it won't be in a safe place in London. You're heading to HMP Durham for life." Chief Inspector O'Reilly stepped out from the far back, deep shadowed corner of the village hall.

"What? Where did you come from?" Walter choked.

"It wasn't me. It was him," whined Roger, as he pointed to Walter.

"We heard the whole thing. Didn't we, everyone?" O'Reilly called to someone in the back.

Lights switched on along the entire length of both sides of the hall. The medical partition the doctor used was propped open along the right side of the wall. From behind the screen stepped Police Constable Jones, two other official-looking men, and finally . . .

"Jim." I screamed so loud I was certain I'd shake the solar panels off the roof.

He ran to my chair, untied my hands, pulled me up, and held me tight.

O'Reilly grabbed Walter and clamped his hands with cuffs. Jonesy did the same with Roger.

With effort I took myself out of Jim's embrace and untied Barbara. "How long have you been in the building, Jim?" I rubbed my face with a hanky he'd given me.

"Not long after you, Dotty." He touched my hair, placing the wayward curl back in place.

"What? You left us tied up thinking we were going to be roast turkey? How could you? How'd you know we were in here? How did you get in? Who are these other men? Why are Jonesy and O'Reilly here? When were you going to rescue us? When they lit the fire?" I couldn't stop the machinegun questioning.

Jim started to chuckle.

Then Barbara.

And Jonesy.

Then me.

The laughter helped ease the tension.

The two official-looking men were introduced as Barbara's MI5 counterparts working the case with her. They took Walter and Roger outside to the waiting police car.

"Mrs. Weathervane?" O'Reilly's brogue sounded like Father O'Malley in *Going My Way*.

"Yes?"

"I'm sorry I had to put you through such a tough ordeal." His blue eyes sparkled like amethysts.

"You are?" I melted like a schoolgirl.

"Taking you and Jim to the station for questioning, coming to the Hare and Hound and saying I was going to arrest you. It was all a ploy to make Reed and Lacey think you were our primary suspects. I knew they were both involved and wanted them to hear me when I came to the pub. Make them relax a bit. Let them think they could get away with everything. Then they'd slip up so we could catch them red-handed. We had Walter convinced he'd gotten away with the murders. But Roger wasn't quite sure."

"But what about the letter? Jonesy quitting? Was that all part of the show?"

"I'm afraid so."

I turned to PC Jones. "I thought you were quitting because you were standing by me to show your support."

Jonesy came up, her brown eyes filled with tenderness. She held my hand. "I'm so sorry, Mrs. Weathervane. I had to go along. It was the only way to trap these two murderers. MI5 have been after them for years, and when Dan and Amy were killed, they contacted us and we started to work with them."

She looked at the area on my wrist burned from rubbing and flinched. "Barbara Swansey was part of the team all along, too. But if I hadn't known what was going on, I would've quit, knowing you and Jim were innocent."

She tenderly placed my hand down by my side. "I'm very sorry you were hurt though. Believe me, we never intended for that to happen."

"Don't worry. My hands will be okay. I'm just thankful to be alive."

"No one ever thought you and Jim had anything to do with these murders," Barbara said.

I turned to O'Reilly. "But how did you know where to find us? Was coming here part of the scheme?" I looked at Barbara. "Did you send me the note from Vivian saying to come? Or was it Roger who wrote it knowing I was friends with Vivian?"

"No, it wasn't me." She rearranged and straightened her skirt and blouse, both wrinkled and askew. "I honestly thought you wrote me the note, and I stopped here to see what you wanted on my way to meeting with these folks. I have no idea how they found us." She turned to O'Reilly. "So how did you know we were here?"

"Why, Mr. Weathervane, of course."

"What?" I grabbed and hugged Jim.

He pulled me off. "Why are you so shocked?"

"I had no idea you heard me say I was coming here or that you ever pay attention when you're out in the garden."

"Of course. I hear you when you talk to me in the garden, or behind the paper, or even when you shoot your questions at me. I don't always acknowledge it, that's all."

"Jim Weathervane, I don't know whether to shoot or kiss you."

"Maybe you'd better kiss him. We don't want any more murders in our village, do we?" Jonesy joked.

I complied.

O'Reilly chuckled. "Tell her why you called us, Mr. Weathervane. You really are the hero on this one."

"Right after you told me you were coming to the hall to meet with Vivian, the phone rang. I came inside to get more water and when I answered it, it was her. She had a question about a party. I knew there was something wrong because she didn't know anything about writing you a note, so I hung up and called Jonesy on her cell. She and the chief inspector were at the house in minutes."

"But how did you get into the building without us knowing?" Barbara asked. "We were in here the whole time."

I chimed in. "We couldn't see much with our heads covered, but I remember hearing creaking after Roger left. Was that you?"

O'Reilly said, "We were hiding around the side of the building. When we saw Roger leave by the back, we sneaked in the front and hid behind the screen. We were hoping Walter would show up and divulge the whole plot while he and Roger were getting ready to kill you. It happened as we hoped, but I'm only sorry you had to be our bait."

Jim said, "Dotty, I knew you and Barbara would be okay as long as the chief inspector and the others were so close. Plus, I would've jumped out if I thought those creeps were going to hurt either of you."

O'Reilly put his hand on my shoulder. "We have everything we need to put those men away for a very long time. And it's all because of you and your husband, Dotty Weathervane."

I moved from O'Reilly and stood with my arm entwined with Jim's. "And to think you didn't want me to get involved." I batted my eyelashes at him.

"I worry about you, that's all." His eyebrows creased upward with the fold of an enormous smile.

Chapter Fifty-Four

"I know you can hear me."

The paper went down.

Jim's questioning eyebrow went up.

"You gave away your secret in the hall last night."

"What secret?"

"You said you hear everything I say, every time. In the garden. Behind the paper. Right?"

"Gee, Dotty, if I thought you were going to use my testimony against me in a court of law or in my own house, I wouldn't have brought the police over to the village hall and saved you." He smiled, lifted the paper, and bobbed the sheets in my face.

Toast was toasting. The kettle steamed then popped off, while I sang Simon's "I'd Do It for Your Love" and tapped my feet. *Ouch. My bunion.* I stopped tapping.

Jim lowered the paper flag.

I stopped singing, stood up, and hugged his neck for a long squeeze until he pulled off my arms and sputtered, "I'd do it for your love, too."

Bliiiing.

"East Lark, 58 1808."

"Can we meet at Molly's?" Kate asked softly.

"Sure. See you there in one hour."

Molly's Tea Leaf's garden was beginning to fill out with sweet peas, green foliage, and overflowing hanging baskets. The center terracotta pot was nearly bursting with the size of its plant. Little tiny buds would sprout lemons and make the whole patio smell like lemonade.

I sat at a table and waited for Kate. She was like Jim, rarely late.

A few minutes later she came in. The redness around her eyes, puffy face, and hanky in her hand good clues she'd been crying.

"I'm sorry I'm late, Dotty." She sat and tucked her skirt under her knees.

"Don't worry about it, Kate. You okay?"

"I guess so. I didn't realize how difficult this whole ordeal has been. I can't believe I almost lost you." She touched the top of my hand. Then pulled it away. "I have a confession though."

"What? What is it?"

Her face flushed. "As much as I am thankful you're okay, I have to say I was sorry it was Walter who was involved. I was beginning to think he and I might have a chance. He seemed like such a good man. So kind. I was looking forward to getting to know him better. Guess I'll never meet someone I can spend my life with, like you and Jim."

"That's not true, Kate. There are plenty of eligible bachelors, but I'm sorry if I got your hopes up about Walter. Believe me, I was disappointed too when he showed up at the village hall. I thought he was going to be our savior when he walked into the place. He sure fooled me."

Kate blew her nose and dried her cheeks.

"He isn't worth the tears, Kate. He was willing to kill Barbara and me without any remorse."

"You're right, of course."

"Let's indulge in some comfort food, shall we? My treat."

We finished our scones with little conversation and left less satisfied than usual with our Molly's Tea Leaf experience.

+ + +

Home again, I turned on the radio and scanned the mess in the kitchen.

Jim knelt in the garden.

Ahh. Home. I love you.

I leaned on the kitchen counter, took off my shoes, and propped open the news.

The paper was filled with details on Walter Reed and Roger Lacey. One article stated that Walter was a magistrate at one time, dismissed from the job because of misdoings but wasn't charged with anything because of lack of evidence.

It turned out Roger Lacey was from London but left there to assume a new identity. "And to hide in our obscure little village of East Lark." I spoke to the four walls.

Roger's name was in fact Albert Lice, and the police had been after him for years. Just reading his name gave me the creeps, made me itch all over and want to scrub my scalp with an intense medicated lotion.

I tossed the papers into the recycling bags and lugged them outside.

At least things can get back to normal.

Stir-fried peppers and other vegetables were in order for dinner. We ate them while watching television. A rare treat since I generally insisted we eat at the table. Instead, we munched as we watched Miss Marple in *A Murder Is Announced*.

We headed up to bed after the ten o'clock news. I was certain there would be no problems with tossing and turning or nightmares tonight. I had had enough bad experiences in broad daylight to last me a lifetime.

Chapter Fifty-Five

I pulled aside the kitchen curtains, opened the French doors, and inhaled a deep breath of warm spring air.

A dove cooed her "good morning," then flew away.

The garden was beyond aesthetically appealing. It was heavenly. No wonder Jim loved to see his garden grow.

I whipped up a batch of steel-cut oatmeal and watched it boil ten minutes, stirring constantly.

"Breakfast's nearly ready," I shouted.

"Dotty? Where are my work clothes?" Jim turned the corner from the stairs and headed into the kitchen dressed in his finer Sunday clothes that I had laid out on the bed for him.

I hummed.

"Did you hear me?" Jim came to the table.

"You're not going to wear your work clothes today."

"And why not?" He let out a low growl.

"Let's just eat our breakfast. Here's the newspaper."

Jim sat and snapped open the paper.

"What's this?" he asked, holding an invitation I'd taped to the inside of the news.

"It's your official invite."

"To what?"

"Read it."

"It says: 'You are invited to enjoy the grand opening of Jim Weathervane's magnificent garden on Saturday at two o'clock.'" Jim looked at me, the questioning eyebrow raised. "That's today. What's this all about, Dotty?"

"I was trying to figure out a way to surprise you, and this was the only way I could think of. I've asked several folks to come and enjoy the beauty you've created outside. I sent these out several days ago."

"Dotty."

"I've put together some games—you know, ice-breakers and such. And I've been collecting the different ingredients for some dishes I'll put together this morning. Then all I need to get are drinks, and of course figure out what I am going to wear."

"Dotty."

"You'll be pleased to know Barbara is coming, along with Jonesy, O'Reilly, and those two young men from MI5. Plus Kate, of course, and the others from the Crime Catchers."

"Dotty."

"So finish up your breakfast. We have work to do."

"Thank you, Dotty."

I stood up, patted his rabbit-eared hair, and kissed his forehead. "Thank *you* for saving my life. I promise never to get involved with another thing like these murders again. Cross my heart and hope to die. Well, never mind that last part."

"Don't make promises you can't keep."

"You're right. Now, please eat your breakfast so you can help set things up. Everybody will be quite envious, especially some of our British friends, when they see your idyllic hideaway."

I headed up the stairs to dress.

Then yelled back. "By the way, what do you think about Chief Inspector O'Reilly and Kate? Wouldn't they be ideal for each other?"

"Dotty."

Chuckle.

Chapter Fifty-Six

Lounging in the summerhouse, Jim and I watched swooping bats catching unseen bugs.

"Thanks, Dotty."

"You're welcome. I'm glad the weather held out. Think it was the nicest day we've had so far this spring. Your garden looked lovely. Alan Titchmarsh would be extremely proud of you, Jim."

The citronella candle was lit between us on the rattan table. Jim's silhouette danced on the wall behind him as he sipped his shandy.

He gave a long, contented sigh. "It was a great party."

I swallowed a sip of elderflower cordial. "I'm glad you enjoyed yourself. And wasn't it wonderful to see everyone having such a good time?"

Jim chuckled. "How about that Vivian?" His laughter deepened as he set down his glass.

"Wasn't it hilarious when she had us move the garden furniture and clear a small space on the grass for folks to try line dancing? Couldn't believe she had you put on a Johnny Cash CD. At first everyone kept bumping into each other, until Fred and Jessica stepped in and gave directions."

"I'm glad Fred's job worked out at the Queen's Treat. Looks like he and Jessica will be running their own pub in the near future."

"Now there's an unexpected happy ending. Who would have ever guessed they would end up doing so well? Gives me hope for others." I sipped my drink.

"Sure does."

"Do you think there's hope for Jake and Lillie?"

Jim picked up his drink and grabbed a handful of leftover nuts. "It's a good sign they came together, don't you think?"

"She looked so pale and thin."

"They talked with each other though, right? Jake's getting a chance to say more than 'yes, dear.'"

"True."

Jim finished his drink and placed the empty glass on the tray. "They're still emotionally raw, but maybe in time they'll be able to share with us, and in the end perhaps they will come out of this stronger as a couple."

"Um. Speaking of a couple."

"I know exactly what you are going to say, Dotty."

"You do?"

"It's pretty obvious. You've been dying to talk about it all evening since everyone left. The grin you've been wearing has been a huge giveaway."

I giggled. "You know me too well, Jim Weathervane."

"Go ahead and say it."

"Kate and Sean O'Reilly make a lovely pair. Sean couldn't stop looking at her, staring as if he was seeing the crown jewels in the London Tower for the first time. They're as sweet together as Prince William and Kate. I think we're going to see the two of them together at many parties. Wonder if they'll name their first child after me?" I giggled.

"Dotty."

"Okay, okay. But you have to admit I was right about him and Kate." My chest pushed out with pride.

"You have to admit you were dead wrong about Walter though." Jim stuck a pin in my pride bubble with the mere mention of Walter's name.

"He sure had me fooled."

"He had us all fooled." Jim paused. "And what about Arty?"

"I know, I know. I was totally wrong about him too. I thought for sure he had something to do with Dan's death when I heard he had a big fight with him before Dan was killed. Arty's a pretty nice guy after all."

The candle flickered.

"Let's not talk about it anymore, okay?"

"Sure, Jim."

"Thanks again for a great party. You're the best. And I'm glad you're safe."

A huge catastrophe had been diverted with the arrest of two murderers, and our little village was slowly getting back to normal. But best of all, my king was crowned in the chess game of marriage.

Plus, there were many things I was looking forward to in the near future. Molly's Tea Leaf, Debenhams' upcoming sale, reading Dorothy L. Sayers' *Murder Must Advertise*, checking out the latest selection of handbags at Age UK, and finally getting to start on my romance novel.

I had new material. This time it would be a lovely woman named Kate and a gorgeous chief inspector glancing at each other over long-stemmed glasses of effervescent bubbly in their hands, after he handcuffed a rogue pub owner and his sidekick magistrate. There was plenty of action from a real-life story for me to use.

Jim burped. "Excuse me. I've had enough to drink and eat to last me quite some time. That tiramisu was wonderful though, Dot. You should make it again sometime. Of course your New York cheesecake was delicious as always."

I purred.

When Jim took the time to speak, he could mold me as if I were a lump of clay being shaped into a beautiful vase. It was a good thing he didn't realize the power he held in his words, or maybe he did and didn't take advantage of how much he could manipulate our relationship. After all, a good marriage was based on mutual love and respect. Not power and control.

The candle petered out.

We grabbed our drinks, picked up the trays filled with the last few stray cups and plates, and headed indoors. Then up the stairs to bed. It was a happy ending to a very happy occasion.

Chapter Fifty-Seven

Another day of bright sunshine was forecast.

The morning news sat on the table. As did a small trowel, gloves, magazines stacked here and there, mail, and leaflets I needed to read through and recycle. There were also paper products and bits and bobs from yesterday's garden party.

Tomorrow was the grand reopening of the village hall and children's playground. A special celebration was to be expected with face painting, balloon races, and various raffles. The bale of fencing was removed, the outhouses were gone, and everything was back to being neat and tidy.

While preparing breakfast I sang "You're the One" at the top of my lungs.

Poached eggs, slices of ham, and hollandaise sauce sat on two pieces of bread, one for Jim and one for me: an eggs benedict favorite family recipe and one never destined to be included on the "biggest loser" list.

BBC played in the background.

My singing and the sound of the classical tunes clashed. But who cared?

Jim came bounding downstairs.

I stacked the papers, news, flyers, and assortment of tools onto a side buffet and placed the special breakfast on the table.

Jim, dressed to work out in the garden, made his Earl Grey.

I softened my singing to a hum.

We sat and ate our meal, slowly, gratefully, listening to the combo of birds in the garden and music on the radio. This was what retirement was supposed to be: lazy mornings, relaxing meals, and long conversations.

Jim grabbed his paper.

Oh well, two out of three wasn't bad.

"Jim?"

"Yes?"

"Now don't get upset."

"I'm going to ignore that, Dotty."

Jim flipped the paper to the next page and shouted, "No, no, no." He jumped and rushed over to the door. At the same time, he crumpled the paper into a massive ball and tossed it onto the top of the recycling bag and pushed down.

"What's the matter?" I asked.

He pointed to the paper. "I don't want you reading it. Do you understand me, Dotty Weathervane?" He said my name with a snap.

"Sure." I went to the bag, pulled out the soccer-sized ball of paper, and unraveled it.

Jim sighed. "Why do you always do the opposite of what I say?"

"Habit." I changed my mind, balled the paper up, and tossed it back into the bag. "If you tell me what's in the paper I won't have to read it. I'm getting smarter in my old-age-pensioner days."

"If I say what's in the paper I want your full guarantee you will not get involved. Agreed? Cross your heart or hope to die?"

"Hm, that's a difficult choice. If I don't agree and you don't read the paper, then I'm not obligated to *not* get involved. But if you do read the—"

"Dotty."

"Okay, tell me what is in the paper you don't want me to know about."

"They are looking for local people to volunteer at the police station."

My ears perked like a fox spotting a rabbit.

I feigned disinterest. "I don't want you to tell me any more."

"Good. Then leave it at that." Jim picked up some of the stacked tools on the side buffet and headed toward the door.

"Dotty Weathervane." The safari hunter look gleamed in his eyes. "Remember what happened the last time." Out he went.

"Yes, dear."

I waited ten seconds then lunged for the paper. Quickly grabbing my leopard-patterned glasses off the table, I slid down under the counter and began reading the details. After all, I couldn't ignore the call of mystery and mayhem, now could I?

About the Author

BEATRICE FISHBACK, originally from New York, lived in the East Anglian area of Great Britain for over twenty years and traveled extensively in the United Kingdom and throughout Europe. She is the author of *Bethel Manor* by Crooked Cat Publishing, *Loving Your Military Man* by FamilyLife Publishing and, with her husband Jim, is the co-author of *Defending the Military Marriage* and *Defending the Military Family.* She has been published in various compilations, magazines and online websites. Beatrice and Jim currently reside in North Carolina where scones are called biscuits and topped with gravy, and tea that is served over ice instead of from a teapot.

Made in the USA
Columbia, SC
12 June 2017